Louis Couperus, And others

Ecstasy

A Study of Happiness

Louis Couperus, And others

Ecstasy
A Study of Happiness

ISBN/EAN: 9783337039905

Printed in Europe, USA, Canada, Australia, Japan

Cover: Foto ©Andreas Hilbeck / pixelio.de

More available books at **www.hansebooks.com**

Ecstasy

A Study of Happiness

By

Louis Couperus

Translated by A. Teixeira de Mattos & John Gray

A New   *Edition*

London H. Henry & Co. Ltd.

93 Saint Martin's Lane W.C.

MDCCCXCVII

How strangely conscious we are these few years
over our translations! And for no special reason
as far as one can see; unless it be that the work
of tricking out in English the mass of foreign
literature which has lately come to us has fallen
mostly into the hands of young people: people
literally too young to remember the days before
the hateful period when translation was looked
upon as hack-work for governesses; people essen-
tially too young to care.

Blatant evidence of this consciousness is found
in the " introduction," without which it is sup-
posed, seemingly, that no foreign novel or drama

can make a perfect bow from an English railway
bookstall; less too in the fact of such introduc-
tions than in their peculiar tone; an unasked
apology which begins by saying that no apology
is needed, and concludes with the comfortable
assurance that writer and reader are both exceedingly intelligent persons.

It is perfectly right and good that the translator of French and Dutch and Norwegian work
should take up his task as a task of high
literature.   Regard to a tithe of the pious
maxims which have been uttered on this subject
spreads an ample field for more conscientious-
ness than is ordinarily found in a translator.
But let not the flattering sense of a worthy and
perhaps self-sacrificing aim encourage in any the
notion that such a view of such work dates only
from the day when the ages decreed that so
exotic a writer as Mr. Ibsen should be given to

the English working classes in a paper wrapper. In all living literatures translations stand on the shelf of honour: GÉRARD DE NERVAL translated HEINE; of LUTHER's bible the astounding assertion has been made that it is greater even than KING JAMES'; in English letters, add to this latter only our CHAPMAN's HOMER, URQUHART'S RABELAIS, THORNLEY's *Daphnis and Chloe*, ROSSETTI's *Italian Poets*, BURTON's *Arabian Nights*, and my point is not far from gained.

Or perhaps the true explanation of the renaissance of right feeling about translation is that editors and publishers nowaday caress themselves that it is the *novel* they are recognising as an important form of artistic expression, to be given the importance and deference which would be due to a work of physical science.

From the point of view of those who seek subtle and gracious expression, or observation even approaching relevancy, the pulpit has ceased to exist. The wordy, stumping opposition, the stage, is but little better off. It might well forego its naïve condescensions towards its elder. Some say it is only sleeping; and point triumphantly to an occasional spasm.

Even the gentle lady Poetry is not seldom seen soiling her white hands and straining her tender muscles, dragging logs to make kennels for unheard-of monsters.

So now, and for a long time to come, it would seem, the novel is the preferred form of artistic utterance. In the novel this century has found that for which it passionately yearned. Among modes of art it is by far the most mobile and variable. The fewness of its restrictions places it with the greatest. It is alike capable of intense complexity and as great simplicity. Here it is wide-armed, embracing a world of men, in all their relations with one another, and all worldly things. There it is preoccupied, glass in hand, with one tiny aspect of one tiny soul. Thought and fancy, intellect and sense, are blended in almost any proportions, to an infinite variety of results.

France with her great ones : BALZAC, FLAUBERT, GONCOURT, MAUPASSANT. Russia has set up a monument against which many a quibble has dashed itself and been broken to pieces. Where in the world is a work so noble, so simple, so austere, as DOSTOIEWSKI'S *Crime and Punishment*?

Holland, with her great vitality, has sprung tardily into activity with a great company of novel writers. These, for the major part, are somewhat restricted in their scope ; and for this reason cannot fairly be compared with the masters of their art. They have very properly turned their attention to a field scarcely broken.   On that they are working patiently, persistently, and it is against probability that they will not find some of the precious metal.   The circle of intellect in Holland is geographically small; and, though dissensions are not wanting either in number or violence, there is a fairly well-defined " school." A " school " in almost all the ideas the word conveys.   With the strong impulses of their age, these young men are for beginning all over again ; for finding out *the* principle, and applying it hot, as it were.   Naturally, the passion to discover the magic principle, the touchstone, tends to keep them awake, and results in work at all events warm and vibrant.   With them there is a good deal of the attitude of the French symbolist poets, the claim to throw over, in the matter of expression, a considerable portion of the tyranny of the grammar book; to use the word that best conveys the impression desired, although such use have not the sanction of custom. New-found freedom is apt to realise itself a little too vividly, and first experiments with a language loosed from the moorings of its tradition are like to be carried out with more impulse than balance. But the temerity of these forerunners has its immediate reward (for, in the end, the language they play tricks with thanks them) in the inevitable youth and cleanness of their language; every word they write is with intention; the *phrase toute faite* is abolished at one stroke, and is no longer present to hamper and choke and sodden. The Dutch school I spoke of is called by itself *Sensitivist*, the word being understood to apply to the method of their literary art, to their manner of seeing and making seen. Of the matter to be treated there is very little left now to fight over. Roughly speaking, *sensitivism* consists, in perhaps its chief element, in exact observation. A person, say, gets a visual impression; a *Sensitivist* would describe what he exactly saw, and not what his intellect, going upon his past experience, would tell him he saw. Or a person hears a sound; the *Sensitivist* tells the impression the sound gave, and later, perhaps, whence the sound proceeded. VOSMEER DE SPIE in *Een Passie*, in other respects too an admirable novel, has carried this principle to a point that gives a shock of surprise at every turn. And to give impressions of sounds, this writer adopts the artifice of using terms of colour. Reflection will show at once the intelligence of this distinction of sense and intellect, and a novel of a *Sensitivist* will show its utility. Most people, knowing that water is transparent, look *through* it: they see water, green, brown, or whatever it may be in its density. Some, with a quicker visual sense, look at its surface, and almost always see beautiful colour.

MR. COUPERUS, the writer of this book *Ecstasy*, is classed as a member of the school I have described. His faith to the tenets of the *Sensitivists* does not soil qualities which would have their delight under any circumstances. MR. COUPERUS is still a young man. This is his third novel; the other two being *Noodlot* and *Eline Vere*, both of which have been translated into English. He has also written a volume of poems : *Orchideeën*.

JOHN GRAY.

ECSTASY:

A STUDY OF HAPPINNESS.

CHAPTER I.

I.

DOLF VAN ATTEMA, for an after-dinner walk, had taken the opportunity of calling on his wife's sister, Cecile Van Even, in the Scheveningen Road. He was waiting in her little boudoir, walking to and fro among the rosewood furniture and the old moiré settees, over and over again, with three or four long steps, measuring the width of the tiny room. On an onyx pedestal, at the head of a *chaise-longue*, burned an onyx

1   1

lamp, glowing sweetly within its lace shade, a great six-petaled flower of light.

Mevrouw was still with the children, putting them to bed, the maid had told him; so he could not see his godson, little Dolf, that evening. He was sorry. He would have liked to go upstairs and romp with Dolf as he lay in his little bed; but he remembered Cecile's request, and his promise of an earlier occasion, when a romp of this sort with his uncle had kept the boy lying awake for hours. So he waited, smiling at his obedience, measuring the little boudoir with his steps—the steps of a firmly-built man, broad and squat, no longer in his first youth, showing symptoms of baldness under his short brown hair, with small blue-grey eyes, kindly and pleasant of glance, and a mouth which was firm and determined, in spite of the smile, in the midst of the ruddy growth of his short Teutonic beard.

A log smouldered on the little hearth of nickel
and gilt, and two little flames flickered discreetly,
—a fire of peaceful intimacy in that twilight
atmosphere of lace-shielded lamplight. Intimacy
and discreetness shed over the whole little room
an aroma as of violets; a suggestion of the
scent of violets nestled, too, in the soft tints of
the draperies and furniture—rosewood and rose
moiré—and hung about the corners of the little
rosewood writing-table, with its silver appoint-
ments, and photographs under smooth glass
frames. Above the writing-table hung a small
white Venetian mirror. The gentle air of
modest refinement, the subdued, almost prudish,
tenderness floating about the little hearth, the
writing-table, and the *chaise-longue*, gliding
between the quiet folds of the fading hangings,
had something soothing, something to quiet the
nerves; so that Dolf presently ceased his work

of measurement, sat down, looked around him,
and finally remained staring at the portrait of
Cecile's husband, the Minister of State, dead
eighteen months back.

After that he had not to wait long before
Cecile came in. She advanced towards him
smiling as he rose from his seat, pressed his
hand, excused herself that the children had
detained her. She always put them to sleep
herself, her two boys, Dolf and Christie, and then
they said their prayers, one beside the other
in their little beds. The scene came back to
Dolf as she spoke of the children ; he had often
seen it.

Christie was not well, he was so listless ; she
hoped it might not turn out to be measles.

There was motherliness in her voice, but she
did not seem a mother as she reclined, girlishly
slight, on the *chaise-longue*, the soft glow be-

hind her of the lamp on its stem of onyx. She was still in the black of her mourning. Here and there the light behind her touched her flaxen hair with a frail golden halo; the loose gown of crape she wore accentuated the girlish slenderness of her figure with the gently curving lines of her long neck and somewhat narrow shoulders; her arms hung with a certain weariness as her hands lay in her lap; gently curving, too, were the lines of her girlish youth of bust and slender waist, slender as a vase is slender; so that she seemed a still expectant flower of maidenhood, scarcely more than adolescent, not nearly old enough to be the mother of her children, her two boys of six and seven.

Her features were lost in the shadow—the lamplight touching her hair with gold—and Dolf could not at first see into her eyes; but presently, as he grew accustomed to the shadow, these shone softly out from the dusk of her features. She spoke in her low-toned voice, a little faint and soft, like a subdued whisper; she spoke again of Christie, of his godchild Dolf, and then asked news of Amélie, her sister.

"We are all well, thank you! You may well ask how we are, we hardly ever see you."

"I so seldom go out," she said as an excuse.

"That is just where you make a mistake; you do not get enough air, enough society. Amélie was only saying so at dinner to-day, and so I came round to ask you to join us to-morrow evening."

"Is it a party?"

"No; nobody."

"Very well, I will come. I shall be very pleased."

"Yes, but why do you never come of your own accord?"

" I can't summon up the energy."

" How do you spend your evenings ? "

" I read, I write, or I do nothing at all. The last is really the most delightful; I only feel myself alive when I do nothing."

He shook his head. " You are a funny girl. You really don't deserve that we should like you as much as we do."

" How ? " she asked, archly.

" Of course it makes no difference to you, you are just as well without us ! "

" You mustn't say that ; it's not true. Your sympathy is very necessary to me, but it takes so much to get me to go out. When I am once in my chair I sit thinking, or not thinking, and I find it difficult to stir."

" What a horribly lazy life ! "

" There it is ! .... You like me so much: can't you forgive me my laziness ? especially when I have promised you to come round to-morrow."

" Very well," he said, laughing. "Of course you are free to live as you choose. We like you just the same, in spite of your neglect."

She laughed, reproached him with using ugly words, and rose slowly to pour out a cup of tea for him. He felt a caressive softness creeping over him, as if he would have liked to stay there a long time, talking and sipping tea in that violet-scented atmosphere of subdued refinement ; he, the man of action, the politician, member of the Second Chamber, every hour of whose day was filled up with committees here and committees there.

" You were saying that you read and wrote a good deal : what do you write ? " he asked.

" Letters."

" Nothing but letters ? "

" I like writing letters. I correspond with my brother and sister in India."

" But that is not the only thing ? "

" Oh, no."

" What else do you write then ? "

" You are growing indiscreet, are you not ? "

" What nonsense ! " he laughed back, as if he were quite within his right. " What is it ? Literature ? "

" No. My diary."

He laughed loudly and joyously. " You keep a diary ! What do you want with a diary ? Your days are all exactly alike."

" Indeed they are not."

He shrugged his shoulders, quite nonplussed; she had always been a riddle to him. She knew this, and loved to mystify him.

" Sometimes my days are very nice, and sometimes very horrid."

" Really!" he said, smiling, looking at her out of his kind little eyes; but he did not understand.

" And so sometimes I have a great deal to write in my diary," she continued.

" Let me see some of it."

" When I am dead."

A mock shiver ran through his broad shoulders. " Brrr! how gloomy!"

" Dead! What is there gloomy about that?" she asked, almost gaily; but he rose to go.

" You frighten me," he said, jestingly. " I must be returning home; I have a great deal of work to do still. So we see you to-morrow?"

" Thanks, yes, to-morrow."

He took her hand, and she struck a little silver gong for him to be let out. He stood looking at her a moment, with a smile in his beard.

" Yes, you are a funny girl, and yet . . . . and

yet we all like you!" he repeated, as if he wished to excuse himself in his own eyes for this sympathy. He bent down and kissed her on the forehead: he was so much older than she.

"I am very glad you all like me," she said. "Till to-morrow, then, goodbye."

He went, and she was alone. The words of their conversation seemed still to be floating in the silence, like vanishing atoms. Then the silence became complete, and Cecile sat motionless, leaning back in the three little cushions of the *chaise-longue,* black in her crape against the light of the lamp, gazing out before her. All around her descended a vague dream as of little clouds, in which faces shone for an instant, from out of which came low voices without logical sequence of words, an aimless confusion of recollection. It was the dreaming of one on whose

brain lay no obsession, either of happiness or
of grief, the dreaming of a mind filled with
peaceful light; a wide, still, grey Nirvana, in
which all the trouble of thinking flows away, and
the thought merely wanders back over former
impressions, taking them here and there, without
selection.   For Cecile's future appeared to her
as a monotonous sweetness of unruffled peace,
where Dolf and Christie grew up into boys,
students, men, while she herself remained nothing
but the mother, for in the unconsciousness of her
spiritual life she did not know herself.   She did
not know that she was more wife than mother,
however fond she might be of her children.
Swathed in the clouds of her dreaming, she did
not feel there was something missing, by reason
of her widowhood; she did not feel loneliness nor
a need of some one beside her, nor regret that
yielding air alone flowed about her, in which her

arms might shape themselves and grope in vain
for something to embrace. The capacity for
these needs was there, but so deep hidden in her
soul's unconsciousness that she did not know of
its existence, that one day it might assert itself
and rise up slowly, up and up, an apparition of
clearer melancholy. For such melancholy as was
in her dreaming seemed to her to belong to the
past, to the memory of the kind husband she
had lost, and never, never, to the present, to an
unrealised sense of her loneliness.

Whoever had told her now that something was
wanting in her life would have roused her indig-
nation; she herself imagined that she had all
she wanted; and highly she valued the calm
contentment of the innocent egoism in which she
and her children breathed, a contentment she
thought complete. When she dreamed, as now,
about nothing in particular—little dream-clouds

fleeing across the field of her imagination, with other cloudlets in the wake—sometimes great tears would well in her eyes, and trickle slowly down her cheek; but to her these were only tears of an unspeakably vague melancholy, a light load upon her heart, barely oppressive, and there for some reason she did not know, for she had ceased to mourn the loss of her husband. In this manner she could pass whole evenings, simply sitting dreaming, never oppressed with herself, nor reflecting how the people outside hurried and tired themselves, aimlessly, without being happy, while she was happy; happy in the cloudland of her dreams.

The hours sped, and her hand was too heavy to reach for the book upon the table beside her; heaviness at last permeated her so thoroughly that one o'clock arrived, and she could not yet decide to get up and go to her bed.

II.

Next evening, when Cecile entered the Van Attemas' drawing-room, slowly, with languorous steps, in the sinuous black of her crape, Dolf advanced towards her and took her hand :

"I hope you will not feel annoyed. Quaerts called, and Dina had told the servants we were at home. I am sorry . . . ."

"It does not matter!" she whispered back, a little irritated nevertheless, in her sensitiveness, at unexpectedly meeting this stranger, whom she did not remember ever to have seen at Dolf's, who now rose from where he had been sitting with old Mrs. Hoze, Dolf's great-aunt, Amélie, and the two daughters, Anna and Suzette. Cecile kissed the old lady, and greeted the rest of the circle in turn, welcomed with a smile by all of them. Dolf introduced :

" My friend Taco Quaerts, ... Mrs. Van Even, my sister-in-law."

They sat a little scattered round the great fire on the open hearth, the piano close to them in the corner, its draped back turned to them, and Jules, the youngest boy, sitting behind it, playing Rubinstein's Romance in Es, and so absorbed that he had not heard his aunt come in.

" Jules . . . . " Dolf cried.

" Leave him alone," said Cecile.

The boy did not reply, and went on playing. Cecile, across the piano, saw his tangled hair and his eyes abstracted in the music. A suspicion of melancholy slowly rose within her; like a weight it climbed up her breast and stifled her breathing. From time to time *forte* notes falling suddenly from Jules' fingers gave her little shocks in her throat, and a strange feeling of uncertainty seemed winding her about as with vague meshes; a feeling not new to her, in which she seemed no longer to possess herself, to be lost and wandering in search of herself, in which she did not know what she was thinking, nor what at this very moment she might say. Something dropped into her brain, a momentary suggestion. Her head sank a little, and, without hearing distinctly, it seemed to her that once before she had heard this romance played so, exactly so, as Jules now played it, very, very long ago, in some former existence ages agone, in just the same circumstances, in this very circle of people, before this very fire; the tongues of the flame shot up with the same flickerings as from the logs of ages back, and Suzette blinked with the same expression she had worn then on that former. . . .

Why was it? that she should be sitting here again now, in the midst of them all? Why

2

should it be? sitting like this round a fire, listening to music? How strange it was, and what
strange things there were in this world ! .... Still,
it was pleasant to be in this company, sweetly
sociable, quiet, without many words, the music
behind the piano dying plaintively away—until
it suddenly stopped. Mrs. Hoze's voice had a
ring of sympathy as she murmured in Cecile's
ear :

"So we are getting you back my child ?
You are coming out from your solitude again ?"

Cecile pressed her hand with a little laugh :

"But have I ever hidden myself? I have
always been at home."

"Yes, but we had to come to you. You have
always remained at home, have you not ?"

"You are not angry with me, are you ?"

"No, dear, of course not ; you have had so
much sorrow."

" Yes; I seem to have lost everything."

How was it she suddenly realised this? She never had had any feeling but of contentment in her own home, among the clouds of her day-dreams, but outside, among other people, she immediately felt that she had lost everything, everything.

" But you have your children . . . ."

" Yes . . . ."

She answered faintly, wearily, with a sense of loneliness, oh! terrible loneliness, like one float-ing aimlessly in space, borne upon thinnest air, in which yearning arms grope in vain.

Mrs. Hoze stood up. Dolf came to take her into the other room to play whist.

" And you too, Cecile?" he asked.

" No; you know I don't . . . ."

He did not press her; there were Quaerts and the girls who would play.

" What are you doing there, Jules ?" he asked,
glancing over the piano.

The boy had remained sitting there, forgotten. He now rose and appeared, tall, grown
out of his strength, with strange eyes.

" What were you doing ?"

" I . . . . I was looking for something . . . . a
piece of music."

" Don't sit moping in that style, my
boy !" growled Dolf kindly, with his deep
voice. " What's become of those cards again,
Amélie ?"

" I don't know," said his wife, looking about
vaguely. " Where are the cards, Anna ?"

" Aren't they in the box with the counters ?"

" No," Dolf grumbled, " nothing is ever where
it should be."

Anna got up, looked, found the cards in the
drawer of a buhl cabinet. Amélie too had risen ;

she stood arranging the music on the piano. She was for ever ordering things in her rooms, and immediately forgetting where she had put them, tidying with her fingers, and perfectly absent in her mind.

"Anna, draw a card too. You can come in later!" cried Dolf from the other room.

The two sisters remained alone with Jules.

The boy sat down on a footstool near Cecile.

"Mamma, do leave my music alone."

Amélie sat down near Cecile.

"Is Christie better?"

"He is a little livelier to-day."

"I am glad. Have you never met Quaerts before?"

"No."

"Really? He comes here so often."

Cecile looked through the open folding-doors at the card table. Two candles stood upon it. Mrs.

Hoze's pink face was lit up clearly, smooth and stately ; her coiffure gleamed silver-grey. Quaerts sat opposite her ; Cecile noticed the round, vanishing silhouette of his head, the hair cut very close, thick and black above the glittering white streak of his collar. His arms made little movements as he threw down a card, or gathered up a trick. His person had something about it of great power, something energetic and sturdy, something of every-day life, which Cecile disliked.

" Are the girls fond of cards ? "

" Suzette is, Anna not so much ; she is not quite so ' brisk.' "

Cecile saw that Anna sat behind her father, staring with eyes which did not understand.

" Do you go out much with them now ? " Cecile asked again.

" Yes, I am obliged to : Suzette likes going

out, but not Anna. Suzette will be a pretty girl,
don't you think so?"

"Suzette is a nasty coquettish thing," said
Jules. "At our last dinner-party . . . ."

He suddenly stopped.

"No, I can't tell you. It's not right to te
tales, is it, auntie?"

Cecile smiled.

"No, certainly it's not."

"I want always to do what is right."

"That is very good."

"No, no!" he said deprecatingly. "Everything
seems to me so bad, do you know. Why is
everything so bad, auntie?"

"But there is much that is good too, Jules."

He shook his head.

"No, no!" he repeated. "Everything is bad.
Everything is very bad. Everything is selfishness.
Just mention something that is not selfish!"

" Parental love ! "

But Jules shook his head again.

"Parental love is ordinary selfishness. Children are a part of their parents, who only love themselves when they love their children."

".Jules ! " cried Amélie, " you talk far too rashly. You know I don't like it : you are much too young to talk like that. One would think you knew everything."

The boy was silent.

" And I always say that we never know anything. We never know anything, don't you think so too, Cecile ? I, at least, never know anything, never . . . ."

She looked round the room absently. Her fingers smoothed the fringe of her chair, tidying up. Cecile put her arm softly round Jules' neck.

III.

It was Quaerts' turn to sit out from the card-table, and although Dolf pressed him to continue playing he rose.

"I want to go and talk to Mrs. Van Even," Cecile heard him say.

She saw him coming towards the room where she still sat with Amélie—Jules sitting at her feet—engaged in desultory talk, for Amélie could never maintain a conversation, always wandering and losing the threads. She did not know why, but Cecile suddenly wore a most serious expression, as if she were discussing very important matters with her sister; though all she said was:

"Jules should really take lessons in harmony, when he composes so nicely . . . ."

Quaerts had approached her; he sat down next

them, with a scarcely perceptible shyness in his manner, a gentle hesitation in the brusque force of his movements.

But Jules fired up.

" No, auntie ; I want to be taught as little as possible. I don't want to learn names and principles and classifications. I could not do it. I only compose like this, like this . . . . " suiting his phrase with a vague movement of his fingers.

" Jules can hardly read, it's a shame ! " said Amélie.

" And he plays so sweetly," said Cecile.

" Yes, auntie ; I remember things, I pick them out on the piano. Ah ! it's not very clever ; it just comes out of myself, you know."

" That is just what is fine."

" No, no ! You have to know the names and principles and classifications. You must have

that in everything. I shall never learn technique;
I can't do anything."

He closed his eyes a moment; a look of
sadness flitted across his restless face.

" You know a piano is so . . . . so big, such a
piece of furniture, isn't it? But a violin, oh, how
delightful ! You hold it to you like this, against
your neck, almost against your heart; it is
almost part of you, and you caress it, like this,
you could almost kiss it ! You feel the soul of
the violin throbbing inside the wood. And then
you only have a string or two, which sing everything. Oh, a violin, a violin ! "

" Jules . . . ." Amélie began.

" And, oh, auntie, a harp ! A harp, like this,
between your legs, a harp which you embrace
with both your arms : a harp is just like an angel,
with long golden hair. Ah, I have never yet
played on a harp ! "

" Jules, leave off!" cried Amélie, angrily.
"You drive me silly with that nonsense! I
wonder you are not ashamed, before Mr.
Quaerts."

Jules looked up in surprise.

" Before Taco ? Do you think I have anything
to be ashamed of, Taco ? "

" Of course not, my boy."

The sound of his voice was like a caress.
Cecile looked at him, astonished; she would
have expected him to make fun of Jules. She
did not understand him, but she disliked him
very much, so healthy and strong, with his
energetic face and his fine expressive mouth, so
different from Amélie and Jules and herself.

" Of course not, my boy."

Jules looked up at his mother contemptuously,
as if he knew better.

" You see! Taco is a good chap." He twisted

his footstool round towards Quaerts, and laid his head against his knee.

" Jules ! "

" Pray let him be, mevrouw."

" Every one spoils that boy . . . ."

" Except yourself," said Jules.

" I ! I ! " cried Amélie, indignantly. " I spoil you out and out ! I wish I knew how not to give way to you ! I wish I could send you to the Indies ! Then you would be more of a man ! But I can't do it ; and your father spoils you too. I don't know what will become of you ! "

" What is to become of you, Jules ? " asked Quaerts.

" I don't know. I mustn't go to college, I am too weak a doll to do much work."

" Would you like to go to the Indies some-day ? "

" Yes, with you . . . . Not alone ; oh, to be alone, always alone ! You will see : I shall always be alone, and it is so terrible to be alone ! "

" But, Jules, you are not alone now," said Cecile, reproachfully.

" Oh, yes, yes, in myself I am alone, always alone . . . ." He pressed himself against Quaerts' knee.

" Jules, don't talk so stupidly," cried Amélie, nervously.

" Yes, yes ! " said Jules, with a sudden half sob. " I will hold my tongue ! But don't talk about me any more ; oh, I beg you, don't talk about me ! " He locked his hands and implored them, with dread in his face. They all stared at him, but he buried his face in Quaerts' knees, as though deadly frightened of something . . . .

Anna had played execrably, to Suzette's despair: she could not even remember the trumps! and Dolf called to his wife:

"Amélie, do come in for a rubber; at least if Quaerts does not wish to. You can't give your daughter very many points, but you are not quite so bad!"

"I would rather stay and talk to Mrs. Van Even," said Quaerts.

"Go and play without minding me, if you prefer, Mr. Quaerts," said Cecile, in a cold voice, as towards some one she utterly disliked.

Amélie dragged herself away with an unhappy face. She, too, did not play a brilliant game, and Suzette always lost her temper when she made mistakes.

"I have so long been hoping to make your

acquaintance, mevrouw, that I should not like to miss the opportunity to-night," answered Quaerts.

She looked at him : it troubled her that she could not understand him. She knew him to be somewhat of a gallant. There were stories in which the name of a married woman was coupled with his. Did he wish to try his blandishments upon her? She had no particular hankering for that sort of pastime; she had never cared for flirtations.

"Why?" she asked, calmly, immediately regretting the word; for her question sounded like coquetry, and she intended anything but that.

"Why?" he repeated. He looked at her in slight embarrassment as he sat near her, with Jules on the ground between them, against his knee, his eyes closed.

" Because . . . . because," he stammered, " because you are my friend's sister, I suppose, and
I used never to see you here. . . ."

She made no answer : in her seclusion she had
forgotten how to talk, and she did not take the
least trouble about it.

"I used often to see you formerly at the
theatre," said Quaerts, " when Mr. Van Even was
still alive."

" At the opera ? " she said.

" Yes."

" Ah ! I did not know you then."

" No."

" I have not been out in the evening for a
long time, on account of my mourning."

" And I always choose the evening to pay my
visits here."

" So it is easily explained that we have never
met."

3

They were silent for a moment.   It seemed to him she spoke very coldly.

"I should like to go to the opera!" murmured Jules with closed eyes.   "Ah no, after all, I think I would rather not."

"Dolf told me that you read a great deal," Quaerts continued.   "Do you keep up with modern literature?"

"A little.   I do not read so very much."

"No?"

"Oh, no.   I have two children, and consequently not much time for it.   Besides, it has no particular fascination for me; life is so much more romantic than any novel."

"So you are a philosopher?"

"I?   Oh, no, I assure you, Mr. Quaerts.   I am the most commonplace woman in the world."

She spoke with her wicked little laugh and her cold voice: the voice and the laugh she employed when she feared lest she should be wounded in her secret sensitiveness, and when therefore she hid herself deep within herself, offering to the outside world something very different from what she really was. Jules opened his eyes and sat looking at her, and his steady glance troubled her.

" You live in a charming place, on the Scheveningen Road."

" Yes."

She realised suddenly that her coldness amounted to rudeness, and she did not wish this, even if she did dislike him. She threw herself back negligently ; she asked at random, quite without concern, merely for the sake of conversation :

" Have you many relations in the Hague ? "

" No ; my father and mother live at Velp, and the rest of my family at Arnhem chiefly. I never fix myself anywhere ; I cannot remain long in one place. I have lived for a considerable time in Brussels."

" You have no occupation, I believe ? "

" No; as a boy my longing was to enter the Navy, but I was rejected on account of my eyes."

Involuntarily she looked into his eyes : small deep-set eyes, the colour of which she could not determine. She thought they looked sly and cunning.

" I have always regretted it," he continued. " I am a man of action. There is always within me the desire of movement. I console myself as best I can with sport."

" Sport ? " she repeated coldly.

" Yes."

" Oh."

" Quaerts is a Nimrod and a Centaur and a Hercules, are you not ? " said Jules.

"Ah, Jules," said Quaerts, with a laugh, "names and theories and classifications. Which class do you really place me in?"

"Among the very, very few people I really love!" the boy answered, ardently, and without hesitation. "Taco, when are you going to give me my riding-lessons?"

"Whenever you like, my son."

"Yes, but you must fix the day for us to go to the riding-school. I won't fix a day, I hate fixing days."

"Well, to-morrow? To-morrow is Wednesday."

"Very well."

Cecile noticed that Jules was still staring at her. She looked at him back. How was it possible that the boy could like this man? How was it possible that it irritated her and not him—all that healthiness, that strength, that power of muscle and rage of sport? She could

make nothing of it; she understood neither
Quaerts nor Jules, and she herself drifted away
again into that mood of half-consciousness, in
which she did not know what she thought, nor
what at that very moment she might say; in
which she seemed to be lost, and wandering in
search of herself.

She rose, tall, frail, in her crape, like a queen
who mourns; touches of gold in her flaxen hair,
where a little jet aigrette glittered like a black
mirror.

"I am going to see who is winning," she said,
and went to the card-table in the other room.
She stood behind Mrs. Hoze, seeming to be
interested in the game, but across the light of
the candles she peered at Quaerts and Jules. She
saw them talking together, softly, confidentially,
Jules with his arm on Quaerts' knee. She saw
Jules looking up, as if in adoration, into the face

of this man, and then the boy suddenly threw his arms around his friend in a wild embrace, while this latter kept him off with a patient gesture.

V.

The next evening Cecile revelled even more than usual in the luxury of being able to stay at home. It was after dinner; she sat on the *chaise-longue* in her little boudoir with Dolf and Christie, an arm thrown round each of them, sitting between them, so young, like an elder sister. In her low voice she was telling them:

"Judah came up to him, and said, O my lord, let me stay as a bondsman instead of Benjamin. For our father, who is such an old man, said to us when we went away with Benjamin: My son Joseph I have already lost; surely he has been torn in pieces by the wild beasts. And if you take this one also from me,

and any harm befall him, I shall become gray
with sorrow, and die. Then (Judah said) I said
to our father that I would be responsible for his
safety, and that I should be very naughty if we
did not bring Benjamin home again. And therefore I pray you, O my lord, let me be your
bondsman, and let the lad go back with his
brethren. For how can I go back to my father
if the lad be not with me. . . ."

"And Joseph, mamma, what did Joseph say ?"
asked Christie. He nestled closely against his
mother, this poor slender little fellow of six, with
his fine golden hair, and his eyes of pale forget-
me-not blue, his little fingers hooking themselves
nervously into Cecile's gown, rumpling the crape.

"Then Joseph could no longer restrain himself, and ordered his servants to leave him;
then he burst into tears, crying, Do you not
know me ? I am Joseph."

But Cecile could not continue, for Christie had thrown himself on her neck in a frenzy of despair, and she heard him sobbing against her.

"Christie! My darling!"

She was greatly distressed; she had grown interested in her own recital and had not noticed Christie's excitement, and now he was sobbing against her in such violent grief that she could find no word to quiet him, to comfort him, to tell him that it ended happily.

"But, Christie, don't cry, don't cry! It ends happily."

"And Benjamin, what about Benjamin?"

"Benjamin returned to his father, and Jacob came down to Egypt to live with Joseph."

The child raised his still wet face from her shoulder and looked at her deliberately.

"Was it really like that? Or are you only making it up?"

" No, really, my darling. Don't, don't cry any more."

Christie grew calmer, but he was evidently disappointed. He was not satisfied with the end of the story; and yet it was very pretty like that, much prettier than if Joseph had been angry, and put Benjamin in prison.

" What a baby, to cry ! " said Dolf. " It was only a story."

Cecile did not reply that the story had really happened, because it was in the Bible. She had suddenly become very sad, in doubt of herself. She fondly dried the child's eyes with her pocket-handkerchief.

" And now, children, bed. It's late ! " she said, faintly.

She put them to bed, a ceremony which lasted a long time; a ceremony with an elaborate ritual of undressing, washing, saying of prayers, tucking in, and kissing. When after an hour she was sitting downstairs again alone, she first realised how sad she felt.

Ah no, she did not know! Amélie was quite right: one never knew anything, never! She had been so happy that day; she had found herself again, deep in the recesses of her most secret self, in the essence of her soul; all day she had seen her dreams hovering about her as an apotheosis; all day she had felt within her consuming love of her children. She had told them stories out of the Bible after dinner, and suddenly, when Christie began to cry, a doubt had arisen within her. Was she really good to her little boys? Did she not, in her love, in the tenderness of her affection for them, spoil and weaken them? Would she not end by utterly unfitting them for a practical life, with which she did not come into contact, but in which the

children, when they grew up, would have to
move? It flashed through her mind: parting,
boarding-schools, her children estranged from
her, coming home big, rough boys, smoking and
swearing, cynicism on their lips and in their
hearts; lips which would no longer kiss her,
hearts in which she would no longer have a place.
She pictured them already with the swagger of
their seventeen or eighteen years, tramping
across her rooms in their cadet's and midship-
man's uniforms, with broad shoulders and a hard
laugh, flicking the ash from their cigars upon
the carpet. Why did Quaerts' image suddenly
rise up in the midst of this cruelty? Was it
chance or a consequence? She could not analyse
it; she could not explain the presence of this
man, rising up through her grief in the atmosphere of her antipathy. But she felt sad, sad,
sad, as she had not felt sad since Van Even's

death; not vaguely melancholy, as she so often felt, but sad, undoubtedly sorrowful at the thought of what must come. Oh! to have to part with her children! And then, to be alone. . . . Loneliness, everlasting loneliness! Loneliness within herself; that feeling of which Jules had such dread; withdrawn from the world which had no charm for her, sunk away alone into all emptiness! She was thirty, she was old, an old woman. Her house would be empty, her heart empty! Dreams, clouds of dreaming, which fly away, which rise like smoke, revealing only emptiness. Emptiness, emptiness, emptiness! The word each time fell hollowly, with hammer strokes, upon her breast. Emptiness, emptiness. . . .

"Why am I like this?" she asked herself. "What ails me? What has altered?"

Never had she felt that word emptiness throb

within her in this way: that very afternoon she had been gently happy, as ordinarily. And now! She saw nothing before her, no future, no life, nothing but broad darkness. Estranged from her children, alone within herself. . . .

She rose up with a half moan of pain, and walked across the boudoir. The discreet half light troubled her, oppressed her. She turned the key of the lace-covered lamp: a golden gleam crept over the rose folds of the silk curtains like glistening water. A strange freshness wafted away something of that scent of violets which hung about everything. A fire burned on the hearth, but she felt cold.

She stood by the little table; she took up a card, with one corner turned down, and read: " T. H. Quaerts." A coronet with five balls was engraved above the name. " Quaerts!" How short it sounded! A name like the smack of a hard hand. There was something bad, something cruel in the name : "Quaerts, Quaerts. . . ."

She threw down the bit of card, angry with herself. She felt cold, and not herself, just as she had felt at the Van Attemas' the evening before.

"I will not go out again. Never again, never!" she said, almost aloud. "I am so contented in my own house, so contented with my life, so beautifully happy. . . . That card! Why should he leave a card? What do I want with his card? . . ."

She sat down at her writing-table and opened her blotting-book. She wished to finish a half-written letter to India; but she was in quite a different mood from when she had begun it. So she took from a drawer a thick book, her diary. She wrote the date, then reflected a moment, tapping her teeth nervously with the silver penholder.

But then, with a little ill-tempered gesture,
she threw down the pen, pushed the book aside,
and, letting her head fall into her hands on the
blotting-book, sobbed aloud.

VI.

Cecile was astonished at this unusually long fit
of abstraction, that it should continue for days
before she could again enter into her usual
condition of serenity, the delightful abode from
which, without wishing it, she had wandered.
But she compelled herself, with gentle compul-
sion, to recover the treasures of her loneliness.
She argued with herself that it would be some
years before she would have to part from Dolf
and Christie: there was time enough to grow
accustomed to the idea of separation. Besides,
nothing had altered either about her or within

her, and so she let the days glide slowly over her, like gently flowing water.

In this way, gently flowing by, a fortnight had elapsed since the evening she spent at Dolf's. It was a Saturday afternoon; she had been working with the children—she still taught them herself—and she had walked out with them; and now she sat again in her favourite room awaiting the Van Attemas, who came every Saturday at half-past four to afternoon tea. She rang for the servant, who lighted the blue flame of methylated spirit. Dolf and Christie were with her; they sat upon the floor on footstools, cutting the pages of a children's magazine to which Cecile subscribed for them. They were sitting quietly and well-bred, like children who grow up in a feeble surrounding, in the midst of too much refinement, too pale, with hair too long and too blonde, Christie especially, whose little temples were

4

veined as if with lilac blood. Cecile stepped by
them as she went to glance over the tea-table,
and the look she cast upon them wrapped the
children in a warm embrace of devotion. She
was in her calmly happy mood; it was so pleasant
that she would soon see the Van Attemas coming
in. She liked these hours of the afternoon when
her silver teakettle hissed over the blue flame.
An exquisite intimacy filled the room; she had
in her long shapely feminine fingers that special
power of witchery, that gentle art of handling
by which everything, over which they glided
merely, acquired a look of herself; an indefinable
something, of tint, of position, of light, which
the things had not until the touch of those
fingers came across them.

There came a ring. She thought it rather
early for the Van Attemas, but she rarely saw
any one else in her seclusion from the outer world

—therefore it must be they. A few moments, however, and Greta came in, with a card. Was mevrouw at home, and could the gentleman see her?

Cecile recognised the card from a distance: she had seen one like it quite recently. Yet she took it up, glanced at it discontentedly, with drawn eyebrows.

What an idea! Why did he do it? What did it mean? But she thought it unnecessary to be impolite and refuse to see him. After all he was a friend of Dolf's. But such persistence . . . .

"Show meneer up," she said.

Greta went, and it seemed to Cecile as though something trembled in the intimacy which filled the room; as if the objects over which her fingers had just passed took another aspect, a look of fright. But Dolf and Christie had not changed; they were still sitting looking at the pictures, with occasional remarks falling softly from their lips.

The door opened, and Quaerts entered the room. He had in still greater measure than before his air of shyness as he bowed to Cecile. To her this air was incomprehensible in him, who seemed so strong, so determined.

"I hope you will not think me indiscreet, mevrouw, taking the liberty to visit you."

"On the contrary, Mr. Quaerts," she said coldly. "Pray sit down."

He sat down and placed his hat on the floor. "I am not disturbing you, mevrouw?"

"Not in the least; I am expecting Mrs. Van Attema and her daughters. You were so polite as to leave a card on me; but you know, I see nobody."

"I knew it, mevrouw. Perhaps it is to that knowledge the indiscretion of my visit is due."

She looked at him coldly, politely, smilingly. There was a feeling of irritation in her. She felt a desire to ask him frankly why he had come.

" How is that ? " she asked, her mannerly smile converting her face into a veritable mask.

" I feared I should not see you for a long time, and I should consider it a great privilege to be allowed to know you more intimately."

His tone was in the highest degree respectful. She raised her eyebrows, as if she did not understand, but the accent of his voice was so very courteous that she could not find a cold word with which to answer him.

" Are those your two children ? " he asked, with a glance towards Dolf and Christie.

" Yes," she replied. " Get up, boys, and shake hands with meneer."

The children approached timidly, and put out their little hands. He smiled, looked at them penetratingly with his small deep-set eyes, and drew them to him.

" Am I mistaken, or is not the little one very like you ? "

" They both resemble their father," she replied.

It seemed to her she had set a shield of mistrust about herself, from which the children were excluded, within which she found it impossible to draw them. It' troubled her that he held them, that he looked at them as he did.

But he set them free, and they went back to their little stools, gentle, quiet, well-behaved.

" Yet they both have something of you," he insisted.

" Possibly," she said.

" Mevrouw," he resumed, as if he had something important to say to her, " I wish to ask you a direct question : tell me honestly, quite honestly, do you think me indiscreet ? "

"Because you pay me a visit? No, I assure you, Mr. Quaerts. It is very polite of you. Only . . . . if I may be candid . . . ."

She gave a little laugh.

"Of course," he said.

"Then I will confess to you that I fear you will find little in my house to amuse you. I see nobody . . . ."

"I have not called on you for the sake of the people I might meet at your house."

She bowed, smiling, as if he had paid her a compliment.

"Of course I am very pleased to see you. You are a great friend of Dolf's, are you not?"

She tried continually to speak differently to him, more coldly, defiantly; but he was too courteous, and she could not do it.

"Yes," he replied, "Dolf and I have known

each other a long time. We have always
been great friends, though we are so entirely
different."

"I like him very much; he is always very
kind to us."

She saw him look smilingly at the little table.
Some reviews were scattered upon it, and a book
or two; among these a little volume of Emerson's
essays, with a paper-cutter inside.

"You told me you did not read much," he
said, mischievously. "I should think . . . ."

And he pointed to the books.

"Oh," said she, carelessly, with a slight shrug
of her shoulders, "a little . . . ."

She thought him tiresome; why should he
remark that she had hidden herself from him?
why, indeed, *had* she hidden herself from
him?

"Emerson," he read, bending forward a little.

" Forgive me," he added quickly. "I have no right to spy upon your pursuits. But the print is so large; I read it from here."

" You are far-sighted ? " she asked, laughing.

" Yes."

His politeness, a certain respectfulness, as if he would not venture to touch the tips of her fingers, placed her more at her ease. She still felt antipathy towards him, but there was no harm in his knowing what she read.

" Are you fond of reading ? " asked Cecile.

" I do not read much: it is too great a pleasure to me for that ; nor do I read all that appears, I am too eclectic."

" Do you know Emerson ? "

" No . . . ."

" I like his essays very much. They look so far into the future. They place one upon such a delightfully exalted level . . . ."

She suited her phrase with an expansive gesture, and her eyes lighted up.

Then she observed that he was following her attentively, with his respectfulness. And she recovered herself; she no longer wished to talk with him about Emerson.

" It is very fine," was all she said, in a most uninterested voice, to close the conversation. " May I give you some tea ? "

" No, thank you, mevrouw ; i never take tea at this time."

" Do you look upon it with so much scorn ? " she asked, jestingly.

He was about to answer, when there was a ring at the bell, and she cried :

" Ah, here they are ! "

Amélie entered, with Suzette and Anna. They were a little surprised to see Quaerts. He said he had wanted to call on Mrs. Van Even. The conversation became general. Suzette was very merry, full of a fancy fair, at which she was going to assist, in a Spanish costume.

"And you, Anna?"

"Oh, no, auntie," said Anna, shrinking together with fright. "Imagine me at a fancy fair! I should never sell anybody anything."

"It is a gift," said Amélie, with a far-away look.

Quaerts rose: he bowed with a single word to Cecile, when the door opened. Jules came in with books under his arm, on his road home from school.

"How do you do, auntie? Hallo, Taco, are you going away just as I arrive?"

"You drive me away," said Quaerts, laughing.

"Ah, Taco, do stay a little longer!" begged Jules, enraptured to see him, in despair that he had chosen this moment to leave.

" Jules, Jules ! " cried Amélie, thinking it was the proper thing to do.

Jules pressed Quaerts, took his two hands, forced him, like the spoilt child that he was. Quaerts laughed the more. Jules in his excitement knocked some books from the table.

" Jules, be quiet ! " cried Amélie.

Quaerts picked up the books, while Jules persisted in his bad behaviour. As Quaerts replaced the last book he hesitated ; he held it in his hand, he looked at the gold lettering : " Emerson. . . ."

Cecile watched him.

" If he thinks I am going to lend it him he is mistaken," she thought.

But Quaerts asked nothing : he had released himself from Jules and said good-bye. With a quip at Jules he left.

VII.

"Is this the first time he has been to see you ?" asked Amélie.

"Yes," replied Cecile. "A superfluous politeness, was it not ?"

"Taco Quaerts is always very correct in matters of etiquette," said Anna, defending him.

"But this visit was hardly a matter of etiquette," Cecile said, laughing merrily. "Taco Quaerts seems to be quite infallible in your eyes."

"He waltzes delightfully !" cried Suzette. "The other day at the Eekhofs dance . . ."

Suzette chattered on ; there was no restraining Suzette that afternoon ; she seemed to hear already the rattling of her castanets.

Jules had a fit of crossness coming on, but he stood still at a window, with the boys.

" You don't much care about Quaerts, do you, auntie ? " asked Anna.

" I do not find him very sympathetic," said Cecile. " You know, I am easily influenced by my first impressions. I can't help it, but I do not like those very healthy, strong people, who look so sturdy and manly, as if they walked straight through life, clearing away everything that stands in their way. It may be a morbid antipathy in me, but I can't help it, that I always dislike a superabundance of robustness. Those strong people look upon others who are not so strong as themselves much as the Spartans used to look upon their deformed children."

Jules could restrain himself no longer.

" If you think that Taco is no better than a Spartan you know nothing at all about him," he said fiercely.

Cecile looked at him, but before Amélie could interpose he continued :

" Taco is the only person with whom I can talk about music, and who understands every word I say. And I don't believe I could talk with a Spartan."

" Jules, how rude you are ! " cried Suzette.

" I don't care ! " he exclaimed furiously, rising suddenly, and stamping his foot. " I don't care ! I won't hear Taco abused, and Aunt Cecile knows it, and only does it to tease me. I think it is very mean to tease a child, very mean. . . . "

His mother and his sisters tried to calm him with their authority. But he seized his books.

" I don't care ! I won't have it ! "

He was gone in a moment, furious, slamming the door, which muttered at the shock. Amélie shook with nervousness.

"Oh, that boy!" she hissed out, shivering. "That Jules, that Jules. . . . "

"It is nothing," said Cecile, gently, excusing him. "He is excitable. . . . "

She had grown a little paler, and glanced towards her boys; Dolf and Christie, who looked up in dismay, their mouths wide open with astonishment.

"Is Jules naughty, mamma?" asked Christie.

She shook her head, smiling. She felt strangely weary, indefinably so. She did not know what it meant; but it seemed to her as if distant perspectives opened up before her eyes, fading away into the horizon, pale, in a great light. Nor did she know what this meant; but she was not angry with Jules, and it seemed to her as if he had not lost his temper with her, but with somebody else. A sense of the enigmatical deepness of life, the unknown of the soul's mystery, like to a fair, bright endlessness, a far-away silvery light, shot through her in a still rapture.

Then she laughed.

"Jules," she said, "is so nice when he gets excited."

Anna and Suzette broke up the circle, and played with the boys, looking at their picture books. Cecile spoke only to her sister. Amélie's nerves were still quivering.

"How can you defend those tricks of Jules?" she asked, in a relenting voice.

"I think it so noble of him to stand up for those he likes. Don't you think so, too?"

Amélie grew calmer. Why should she be disturbed if Cecile was not?

"Oh yes, yes. . . ." she replied. "I don't know. He has a good heart I believe, but he is so un-manageable. But, who knows? . . . perhaps the

5

fault is mine; if I understood better, if I had more tact . . . . ”

She grew confused; she sought for something more to say, found nothing, wandering like a stranger through her own thoughts. Then, suddenly, as if struck by a ray of certain knowledge, she said . . . .

“ But Jules is not stupid. He has a good eye for all sorts of things, and for persons too. For my part, I believe you judge Taco Quaerts wrongly. He is a very interesting man, and a great deal more than a mere sportsman. I don’t know what it is, but there is something about him different from other people, I couldn’t say precisely what . . . . ”

She was silent, seeking, groping.

“ I wish Jules got on better at school. He is not stupid, but he learns nothing. He has been two years now in the third class. The boy has no application. He makes me despair of him."

She was silent again, and Cecile too remained silent.

"Ah," said Amélie, "I daresay it is not his fault. Perhaps it is my fault. Perhaps he takes after me. . . . "

She looked straight before her : sudden irrepressible tears filled both her eyes, and fell into her lap.

"Amy, what is the matter?" asked Cecile, kindly.

But Amélie had risen, so that the girls, who were still playing with the children, might not see her tears. She could not restrain them, they streamed down, and she hurried away into the adjacent drawing-room, a big room, where Cecile never sat.

"What is the matter, Amy?" repeated Cecile.

She threw her arms about her sister, made her sit down, pressed her head against her shoulder.

"How do I know what it is?" sobbed Amélie. "I do not know, I do not know .... I am wretched because of that feeling in my head. After all, I am not mad, am I? Really, I don't feel mad, or as if I were going mad! But I feel sometimes as if everything had gone wrong in my head, as if I couldn't think. Everything runs through my brain. It is a terrible feeling!"

"Why don't you see a doctor?" asked Cecile.

"No, no, he might tell me I was mad, and I am not. He might try to send me into an asylum. No, I won't see a doctor. I have every reason to be happy otherwise, have I not? I have a kind husband and dear children; I have never had any great sorrow. And yet I sometimes feel deeply miserable, unreasonably miserable! It is always as if I wanted to reach some place and could not succeed. It is always as if I were hemmed in. . . . "

She sobbed violently; a storm of tears rained down her face. Cecile's eyes, too, were moist; she liked her sister, she felt for her. Amélie was only ten years her senior, and already she had something of an old woman about her, withered, mean, her hair growing grey at the temples, under her veil.

"Cecile, tell me, Cecile," she said suddenly, through her sobs, "do you believe in God?"

"Of course, Amy."

"I used to go to church, but it was no use. . . . I don't go any more. . . . Oh, I am so unhappy! It is very ungrateful of me. I have so much to be grateful for. . . . Do you know, sometimes I feel as if I would like to go at once to God, all at once!"

" Pray, Amy, do not excite yourself so."

" Ah, I wish I were like you, so calm. Do you feel happy ? "

Cecile nodded, smiling. Amélie sighed; she remained lying a moment with her head against her sister's shoulder. Cecile kissed her, but suddenly Amélie started :

"Be careful," she whispered, " the girls might come in here. They . . . . they need not see that I have been crying."

Rising, she arranged herself before the looking-glass, carefully dried her veil with her handkerchief, smoothed the strings of her bonnet.

" There, now they won't know," she said. " Let us go in again. I am quite calm. You are a dear girl. . . . "

They went into the little room.

" Come, girls, we must go home," said Amélie, in a voice which was still unsettled.

"Have you been crying, mamma?" asked Suzette immediately.

"Mamma was a little upset about Jules," said Cecile quickly.

VIII.

Cecile was alone; the children had gone up stairs to get ready for dinner. She tried to get back her distant perspectives, fading into the pale horizon; she tried to get back the silvery endlessness which had shot through her as a vision of light. But it confused her too much: a kaleidoscope of recent petty memories: the children, Quaerts, Emerson, Jules, Suzette, Amélie. How strange, how strange was life! . . . . The outer life; the coming and going of people about us; the sounds of words which they utter in accents of strangeness; the endless changing of phenomena; the concatenation of those pheno-

mena, one with the other; strange, too, the
presence of a soul somewhere, like a god within
us, never in its essence to be known, save by
itself. Often, as now, it seemed to Cecile that
all things, even the most commonplace, were
strange, very strange; as if nothing in the world
were absolutely commonplace; as if everything
were strange together; the strange form and
exterior expression of a deeper life, that lies
hidden behind everything, even the meanest
objects; as if everything displayed itself under
an appearance, a transitory mask, while under-
neath lay the reality, the very truth. How
strange, how strange was life . . . . For it
seemed to her as if she, under all the ordinariness
of that afternoon tea-party, had seen something
very extraordinary; she did not know what, she
could not express nor even think it; it seemed
to her as if beneath the coming and going of

those people there had glittered something: reality, ultimate truth beneath the appearance of their happening to come to take tea with her.

"What is it? What is it?" she asked. "Am I deluding myself, or is it so? I feel it so. . . ."

It was very vague, and yet so very clear. . . . It seemed to her as if there was an apparition, a haze of light behind all that had happened there. Behind Amélie, and Jules, and Quaerts, and that book he had just held in his hand. . . . Did those apparitions of light mean anything, or. . . .

But she shook her head.

"I am dreaming, I am giving way to fancy," she laughed within herself. "It was all very simple; I only make it complicated because I take pleasure in doing so."

But so soon as she thought this, there was

something that denied the thought absolutely ; an intuition which should have made her guess the essence of the truth, but which did not succeed in doing so. For sure there was something, something behind all that, hiding away, lurking as the shadow lurks behind the thing. . . .

Her thought still wandered over the company she had had, then halted finally at Taco Quaerts. She saw him sitting there again, bending slightly forward towards her, his hands locked together hanging between his knees, as he looked up to her. A barrier of aversion had stood between them like an iron bar. She saw him sitting there again, though he was gone. That again was past ; how quickly everything moved ; how small was the speck of the present !

She rose, sat down at her writing-table, and wrote :

"Beneath me flows the sea of the past, above

me drifts the ether of the future, and I stand
midway upon the one speck of reality; so small
that I must press my feet firmly together not
to lose my hold. And from the speck of my
present my sorrow looks down upon the sea, and
my longing up to the sky.

" It is scarcely life to stand upon this ledge, so
small that I hardly appreciate it, hardly feel it
beneath my feet; and yet to me it is the one
reality. I am not greatly occupied about it : my
eyes only follow the rippling of those waves
towards the distant haven, the gliding of those
clouds towards the distant spheres : vague mani-
festations of endless mutability, translucent
ephemeras, visible incorporeities. The present is
the only thing that is, or rather that seems to
be ; but not the sea below nor the sky above ;
for the sea is but memory, and the air but an
illusion. Yet memory and illusion are every-

thing : they are the wide inheritance of the soul, which alone can escape from the speck of the moment to float away upon the sea towards the haven which for ever retreats, to rock upon the clouds towards the spheres which retreat and retreat. . . ."

Then she reflected. How was it she had written so, and why? How had she come to do it? She went back upon her thoughts : the present, the speck of the present, which was so small . . . . Quaerts, Quaerts' very attitude, rising up before her just now. Was it in any way owing to him that she had written down those sentences? The past a sorrow; the future an illusion. . . . Why, why illusion ?

" And Jules, who likes him. . . ." she thought. " And Amélie, who spoke of him . . . . but she knows nothing. . . . What is there in him, what lurks behind him, what is he himself? Why did he come here? Why do I dislike him so? Do I dislike him? I cannot see into his eyes. . . ."

She would have liked to do this once; she would have liked to make sure that she disliked him, or that she did not—whichever it might be. She was curious to see him once more, to know what she would think and feel about him then. . . .

She had risen from her writing-table, and now lay at full length on the *chaise-longue*, her arms folded behind her head. She no longer knew what she dreamt, but she felt peacefully happy. Dolf and Christie were coming down the stairs. They came in, it was dinner-time.

"Jules was naughty just now, really, was he not, mamma?" asked Christie again, with a doubtful face.

She drew the frail little fellow softly to her,

took him tightly in her arms, and gently kissed his moist, pale mouth.

" No, really not, my darling !" she said. " He was not naughty, really. . . ."

CHAPTER II.

I.

CECILE passed through the long hall, which was almost a gallery : servants stood by the doorway, a hum of voices came from behind it. The train of her dress rustled against the leaves of a palm fern, and this sound gave a sudden jar to the strung cords of her sensitiveness. She was a little nervous; her eyelids quivered slightly, and her mouth had a very earnest fold.

She walked in ; there was much light, but very subdued, the light of candles. Two officers stepped aside for her as she hesitated. Her eyes glanced quickly round in search of Mrs. Hoze. She observed her standing with two or three of

her guests, with her grey hair, with her kindly
and yet haughty expression, rosy and smooth,
with scarcely a wrinkle. Mrs. Hoze advanced
towards her.

" How charming of you not to have disappointed me ! " she said, pressing Cecile's hand,
effuse in the urbane amiability of her hospitality.

She introduced Cecile here and there ; Cecile
heard names, which immediately afterwards es-
caped her.

"General, allow me . . . . Mrs. Van Even,"
Mrs. Hoze whispered, and left her, to speak to
some one else. Cecile answered the general
cursorily. She was very pale, and her eyelids
quivered more and more. She ventured to throw
a glance round the room.

She stood next to the general, forcing herself
to listen, in order not to give strikingly silly
replies ; she was tall, slender, and straight, her

shoulders, blonde as marble in sunlight, blossoming out of a sombre vase of black: fine black training tulle, sprinkled over with small jet spangles: glittering black upon dull transparent black. A girdle with tassels of jet, hanging low, was wound about her waist. So she stood, blonde; blonde and black, a little sombre amid the warmth and light of other toilettes; and, for unique relief, two diamonds in her ears, like dewdrops.

Her thin suède-covered fingers trembled as she manipulated her fan, a black tulle transparency, on which the same jet spangles glittered with black lustre. Her breath came short behind the strokes of the translucent fan as she talked with the general, a spare, bald, distinguished man, not in uniform, but wearing his decorations.

Mrs. Hoze's guests walked about, greeting one another here and there, a continuous humming

6

of voices. Cecile saw Taco Quaerts come up to her; he bowed before her; she bowed coldly in return, not offering him her hand. He lingered a moment by her, exchanged a single word, then passed on, greeting other acquaintances.

Mrs. Hoze had taken the arm of an old gentleman; a procession formed itself slowly. The servants threw back the doors; a table glittered beyond. The general offered Cecile his arm, and she looked behind her with a slow movement of her neck. She closed her eyelids a moment, to prevent the quivering which oppressed them. Her eyebrows contracted slightly with a disappointment, but smilingly she laid the tips of her fingers on the general's arm, and with her closed fan smoothed away a crease from the tulle of her train.

II.

When Cecile was seated she found Quaerts sitting on her right. Her disappointment vanished, the disappointment she had felt at not being taken in to dinner by him; but when she addressed him her look remained cold, as usual. She had what she wished; the expectation with which she had accepted this invitation was now fulfilled. Mrs. Hoze had seen Cecile at the Van Attemas, and had gladly undertaken to restore the young widow to society. Cecile knew that Quaerts was one of Mrs. Hoze's visitors; she had heard from Amélie that he was among the invited, and she had accepted. That Mrs. Hoze, remembering Cecile had met Quaerts before, had placed him next to her, was easy to understand.

Cecile was very inquisitive about herself. How would she feel? At least interested; she could

not disguise that from herself. She was certainly interested in him, remembering what Jules
had said, what Amélie had said. She now felt
that behind the mere sportsman there lurked
another, whom she longed to know. Why?
What concern was it of hers? She did not know;
but in any case, as a matter of simple curiosity,
it awoke her interest. At the same time she
remained on her guard; she did not think his
visit had been strictly in order, and there were
stories in which the name of a married woman
was coupled with his.

She succeeded in freeing herself from her conversation with the general, who seemed to feel
himself called upon to entertain her, and it was
she who first spoke to Quaerts.

" Have you begun to give Jules his riding-
lessons?" she asked with a smile.

He looked at her, evidently a little surprised

at her voice and her smile, which were both new to him. He returned a bare answer:

"Yes, mevrouw, we were at the riding-school yesterday. . . ."

She thought him clumsy to let the conversation drop like that, but he inquired with that slight shyness which became a charm in him who was so manly:

"So you are going out again, mevrouw?"

She thought—she had thought so before also—that his questions were such as were never asked. There was always something strange about them.

"Yes," she replied simply, not knowing indeed what else to say.

"Pardon me. . . ." he said seeing that his words embarrassed her. " I asked, because. . . ."

"Because?" she repeated, surprised.

He took courage, and explained: "When Dolf spoke of you he used always to say that you

lived quietly. . . . Now I could never picture
you to myself returned among society; I had
formed an idea of you, and now it seems to me
that idea was a mistaken one."

"An idea?" she asked. "What idea?"

"Perhaps you will not be pleased when I tell
you. Perhaps even as it is you are displeased
with me!"

"I have not the slightest reason to be either
pleased or displeased with you. But tell me
what was your idea. . . ."

"You are interested in it?"

"If you will tell me candidly, yes. But you
must be candid!" and she threatened him with
her finger.

"Then. . . ." he began, "I thought of you as
a woman of culture, desirable as an acquaintance—I still think all that—*and* as a woman
who cared nothing for the world beyond her own

sphere ;—and that . . . . I can now think no longer. I should like to say, and risk your thinking me very strange, that I am sorry no longer to be able to think of you in that way. I would almost have preferred not to meet you here. . . ."

He laughed, perhaps to soften what was strange in his words. She looked at him with amazement, her lips half-opened, and suddenly it struck her that for the first time she was looking into his eyes. She looked into his eyes, and she saw that they were a dark, dark grey around the black of the pupil. There was something in his eyes, she could not say what, but something magnetic, as if she could never again take away her own from them.

" How strange you can be sometimes ! " she said, the words coming intuitively.

" Oh, I beg you, do not be angry," he almost

implored her. " I was so glad when you spoke kindly to me. You were a little distant to me when last I saw you, and I should be so sorry if I angered you. Perhaps I am strange, but how could I possibly be commonplace with you ? How could I possibly, even if you were to take offence ? .... *Have* you taken offence ? "

" I ought to, but I suppose I must forgive you, if only for your candour ! " she said, laughing. " Otherwise your remarks are anything but gallant."

" And yet I intended no unmannerliness."

" I suppose not."

She remembered that she was at a big dinner-party. The guests ranged before and around her ; the footmen waiting behind ; the light of the candles sparkling on the silver and touching the glass with all the hues of the rainbow ; on the table prone mirrors like sheets of water, surrounded by flowers, little lakes amidst moss-roses and lilies of the valley. She sat silent a moment, still smiling, looking at her hand, a pretty hand, like a white precious thing upon the tulle of her gown; one of the fingers bore several rings, scintillating sparks of blue and white.

The general turned to her again; they exchanged a few words; the general was delighted that Mrs. Van Even's right-hand neighbour kept her entertained, and so enabled him to get on quietly with his dinner. Quaerts turned to the lady on his right.

Both were pleased when they were able to resume their conversation.

" What were we talking about just now? " she asked.

" I know! " he replied mischievously.

" The general interrupted us. . . ."

" You were *not* angry with me ! "

"Oh yes," she replied, laughing softly. " It
was about your idea of me, was it not ? Why
could you no longer conceive me returned to
society ? "

" I thought you had grown a person apart."

" But why ? "

" From what Dolf said, from what I thought
myself, when I saw you."

" And why are you sorry now that I am not ' a
person apart ' ? " she asked, still laughing.

" From vanity : because I have made a mistake.
And yet, perhaps I have not made a mistake. . . ."

They looked at one another, and both, whatever
else they might have been thinking, now thought
the same thing : namely, that they must be
careful with their words, because they were
speaking of something very delicate and tender,
something as frail as a soap-bubble, which could

easily break if they spoke of it too loudly, the mere breath of their words might be sufficient. Yet she ventured to ask :

"And why .... do you believe .... that perhaps .... you are not mistaken ? "

" I don't quite know. Perhaps because I wish it so. Perhaps, too, because it is so true as to leave no room for doubt. Ah, yes, I am almost sure that I had judged rightly. Do you know why? Because otherwise I should have hidden myself and been matter-of-fact, and I find this impossible with you. I have given you more of my very self in this short moment than I have given people whom I have known for years in the course of all those years. Therefore, surely you must be a person apart."

" What do you mean by 'a person apart'? "

He smiled, he opened his eyes, she looked into them again, deeply into them.

" You understand quite well what I mean," he said.

Fear for the delicate thing that might break came between them again. They understood one another as with a freemasonry of comprehension. Her eyes were magnetically held upon his.

" You are very strange ! " she said again, automatically.

" No," he said, calmly, shaking his head, his eyes upon hers. " I am certain that I am not strange to you, although at this moment you may think so."

She was silent.

" I am so glad to be able to talk to you like this ! " he whispered. " It makes me very happy. And see, no one knows anything of it. We are at a big dinner: the people next to us catch our words: yet there is no one among them understands us, or grasps the subject of our conversation. Do you know the reason of this ? "

" No," she murmured.

" I will tell you ; at least I think it is this : perhaps you know better, for you must know things better than I, you so much subtler. I personally believe that each person has an environment about him, an atmosphere, and that he meets other people who have environments or atmospheres about them, sympathetic or antipathetic to his own."

"That is pure mysticism ! " she said.

" No," he replied; " it is very simple. When the two circles are antipathetic, each repels the other ; but when they are sympathetic, then they glide one over the other with smaller or larger folds of sympathy. In rarer cases the circles almost coincide, but they always remain separate .... Do you really think this so mystical ? "

"One might call it the mysticism of sentiment. But I have thought something of the sort myself. . . ."

"Yes, yes, I can understand that," he continued, calmly, as if he expected it. " I believe those around us could not understand what we are saying, because we two alone have sympathetic environments. But my atmosphere is of grosser texture than your own, which is very delicate."

She was silent again, remembering her aversion to him—did she still feel that?

"What do you think of my theory?" he asked.

She looked up ; her white fingers trembled in the tulle of her gown. She made a poor effort to smile.

"I think you go too far ! " she stammered.

"You think I rush into hyperbole ? "

She would have liked to say yes, but could not. " No," she said ; " not that."

" Am I wearying you ? . . . ."

She looked at him ; deep into his eyes. She made a gesture to say no. She would have liked to say that he was too unconventional ; but she could not find words. A drowsiness oppressed her whole being. The table, the people, the whole dinner seemed to her as through a haze of light. When she recovered she saw that a pretty woman sitting opposite, who now looked another way out of politeness, was gazing at her steadfastly. She did not know why this interested her, but she asked Quaerts : " Who is that lady over there, in pale blue, with dark hair ? "

She saw that he started.

" That is young Mrs. Hijdrecht ! " he said calmly, his voice a little raised.

She turned pale ; her fan flapped nervously to and fro.

He had named the woman rumour said to be his mistress.

III.

It seemed to Cecile as though that delicate, frail thing, that soap-bubble, had burst. She wondered if he had spoken to that dark-haired woman also of circles of sympathy. So soon as she was able, Cecile observed Mrs. Hijdrecht. She had a warm, dull-gold complexion, fiery dark eyes, a mouth as of fresh blood. Her dress was cut very low ; her throat and the slope of her breast came out insolently handsome, brutally luscious. A row of diamonds encircled her neck with a narrow line of white brilliancy.

Cecile felt ill at ease. She looked away from the young woman, and turned to Quaerts, drawn magnetically towards him. She saw a cloud of melancholy stealing over the upper half of his face ; over his forehead and his eyes, in which appeared a slight look of age. And she heard him say :

"What do you care about that lady's name ; we were just in the middle of such a charming conversation. . . . "

She too felt sad now; sad for the soap-bubble that had burst. She did not know why, but she felt pity for him ; sudden, deep, spontaneous pity.

"We can resume our conversation," she said softly.

"Ah no, do not let us take it up where we left it," he rejoined with feigned airiness. " I had become too serious."

He spoke of other things : she answered little, and their conversation languished. They each

7

occupied themselves with their neighbours. The
dinner came to an end. Mrs. Hoze rose, took the
arm of the gentleman next her. The general
escorted Cecile to the drawing-room, in the slow
procession of the others.

The ladies remained alone, the men went to
the smoking-room with young Hoze. Cecile
saw Mrs. Hoze coming towards her. She asked
her if she had not been wearied at dinner; they
sat down by one another, in a confidential *têle-à-
léte.*

Cecile compelled herself to reply to Mrs. Hoze,
but she would gladly have gone elsewhere, to weep
quietly, because everything passed so quickly,
because the speck of the present was so small.
Past, again, was the sweet charm of their conversation at dinner about sympathy, a fragile
intimacy amid the worldly splendours about them.
Past that moment, never, never to return : life

sped over it with its onflowing, a flood of all-
obliterating water. Oh, the sorrow of it ; to think
how quickly, like an intangible perfume, everything speeds away, everything that is dear to
us. . . .

Mrs. Hoze left her ; Suzette Van Attema came
to talk to Cecile. She was in pink, and shining
in all her aspect as if gold dust had rained over her,
upon her movements, her eyes, her words. She
spoke volubly to Cecile, telling interminable tales,
to which Cecile did not always listen. Suddenly,
through Suzette's prattling, Cecile heard the
voices of two women whispering behind her ; she
only caught a word here and there :

" Emilie Hijdrecht, you know. . . ."

"Only gossip, I think ; Mrs. Hoze does not
seem to heed it. . . ."

" Ah ! I am afraid I know better."

The voices were lost in the hum of others.

Cecile just caught a sound like Quaerts' name. Suzette asked suddenly :

" Do you know young Mrs. Hijdrecht, auntie ? "

" No."

" Over there, with the diamonds. You know, they talk about her and Quaerts. Mamma does not believe it. He is a great flirt in any case. You sat next to him, did you not ? "

Cecile suffered severely in the secrecy of her sensitiveness. She shrank entirely within herself, doing all she could to appear different from what she was. Suzette saw nothing of her discomfiture.

The men returned. Cecile looked to see whether Quaerts would speak to Mrs. Hijdrecht. But he wholly ignored her presence, and even, when he saw Suzette sitting with Cecile, came over to them to pay a compliment to Suzette, to whom he had not yet spoken.

It was a relief for Cecile when she was able to go. She longed for solitude, to recover herself, to return from her abstraction. In her brougham she scarcely dared breathe, fearful of something she could not say what. When she reached home she felt a stifling heaviness which seemed to paralyse her, and with difficulty she passed up the stairway to her dressing-room.

And yet, as she stepped, there fell over her, as from the roof of her house, a haze of protecting safety. Slowly she went up, her hand, holding a long glove, pressing the velvet banister of the stairway. She felt as if she were about to swoon.

" But, my God . . . . I am fond of him, I love him, I love him!" she whispered between her trembling lips, with sudden amazement.

It was as in a rhythm of astonishment that she wearily mounted the stairway, higher and higher, in a still surprise of sudden light.

"But I am fond of him, I love him, I love him!"

It sounded like a melody through her weariness.

She reached her dressing-room, where Greta had lighted the gas; she dragged herself inside. The door of the nursery stood half open; she entered it, threw up the curtain of Christie's little bed, fell on her knees, and looked at the child. The boy partly awoke, still in the warmth of deep sleep; he crept a little from between the sheets, laughed, threw his arms about Cecile's bare neck.

"Mamma dear!"

She pressed him tightly in the embrace of her slender white arms; she kissed his raspberry mouth, his drowsed eyes. Meantime the refrain sang on in her heart, right across the weariness, which broke, as it were, by the cot of her child:

" I am fond of him, I love him, I love him, I love him. . . . ! "

IV.

The mystery! Suddenly, on the staircase, it had beamed open before her in her soul, like a great flower of light, a mystic rose with glistening leaves, into whose golden heart she now looked for the first time. The analysis of which she was so fond was no longer possible : this was the Enigma of Love, the eternal Enigma, that had beamed open within her, transfixing with its rays the width and breadth of her soul, in the midst of which it had burst forth like a sun in the universe ; it was no longer of use to ask, Why, why; it was no longer of use to ponder and dream on it; it could only be accepted as the inexplicable phenomenon of the soul; it was a creation of sentiment, of which the god who created it would be as impossible to find in the essence of his reality as the God who had created the world out of chaos. It was the light breaking forth from the darkness; it was, heaven disclosed above the earth. It existed, it was reality and no chimera; for it was wholly and entirely within her; a sudden, incontestable, everlasting truth, a felt fact, so real in its ethereal incorporeity that it seemed to her as if before that moment she had never known, never thought, never felt. It was the beginning: the opening out of herself, the dawn of her soul's life, the joyful miracle, the miraculous inception of love, Love in the midst of her soul a centre sun.

She passed the days which followed in self-contemplation, wandering through her dreams as through a new country, rich with great light, where distant landscapes paled into light, fantastic, like meteors in the night, quivering in incandescence upon the horizon. It seemed to her as though she, a blithe, pious pilgrim, progressed along paradisial oases towards those distant scenes, there to find still more: the Goal. . . . Only a little while ago her prospect had been but narrow and forlorn—her children gone from her, her loneliness wrapping her about like a night—and now, now she saw before her a long road, a wide horizon, glittering the whole way in light; nothing but light. . . .

That *was*, all that *was*! It was no fine poet's dream; it existed, it gleamed in her heart like a sacred jewel, like a mystic rose with stamina of light! A freshness as of dew fell over her, over her whole life: over the life of her senses: over the life of outward appearances: over the life of her soul: over the life of the truth indwelling. The world was new, fresh with

young dew, the very Eden of Genesis, and her
soul was a soul of newness, born anew in a
metempsychosis of greater perfection, of closer
approach to the ideal, that distant Goal—there,
far away, hidden like a god in the sanctity of
its ecstasy of light, in the radiance of its own
being.

V.

Cecile did not go out for a few days; she saw
nobody. One morning she received a note; it
ran :

"MEVROUW,

"I do not know if you were offended at my
mystical utterances. I cannot recall distinctly
what I said, but I remember that you told me
that I was going too far. I hope you have not
taken my indiscretion amiss. It would be a
great pleasure to me to come to see you. May

I hope that you will permit me to call on you this afternoon?

"With most respectful regards,

"QUAERTS."

As the bearer was waiting for a reply, she wrote back in answer:

"DEAR SIR,

"I shall be pleased to see you this afternoon.

"CECILE VAN EVEN."

When she was left alone she read the note over and over again; she looked at the paper with a smile, looked at the handwriting.

"How strange," she thought. "This note, and everything that happens. How strange everything is, everything, everything!"

She remained dreaming a long time, with the

note in her hand. Then she carefully folded it up,
rose, walked up and down the room, sought in a
bowl full of visiting cards, taking out two which
she looked at for a long time. " Quaerts. . . . "
The name sounded differently from before. . . .
How strange it all was! And finally she locked
away the letter and the two cards in a little
empty drawer of her writing-table.

She stayed at home, and sent the children
out with the nurse. She hoped no one else
would call, neither Mrs. Hoze nor the Van
Attemas. And staring before her she reflected
a long, long time. There was so much she did
not understand: properly speaking she understood nothing. As far as she was concerned,
she had fallen in love ; there was no analysing
that, it must simply be accepted. But he,
what did he feel, what were his emotions ?

Her earlier antipathy ? Sport . . . . he was fond

of sport she remembered. . . . His visit, which was an impertinence. . . . He seemed to wish now to atone, not to call again without her permission. His mystical conversation at the dinner-party. . . . And Mrs. Hijdrecht. . . .

" How strange he is," she reflected. " I cannot understand him ; but I love him, I cannot help it. Love, love . . . . how strange that it should exist ! I never realised that it existed ! I am no longer myself : I am becoming some one else ! Why does he wish to see me ? . . . . And how singular : I have been married, I have two children ! How singular, that I should have two children ! I feel just as if I had none. And yet, I am so fond of my little boys ! But the other thing is so beautiful, so bright, so transparent, as if that alone were truth. Perhaps love *is* the only truth. . . . It is as if everything in and about me were turning to crystal ! "

She looked around her, surprised and troubled that her surroundings should have remained the same : the rosewood furniture, the folds of the curtains, the withered landscape of the Scheveningen Road outside. But it snowed, still and softly, with great slow flakes which fell heavily, as if they would purify the world. The snow was fresh and new, but yet the snow was not real nature to her, who always saw her distant landscape, like a *fata morgana*, quivering in pure incandescence of light.

At four o'clock he came. She saw him for the first time since the self-revelation which had flashed upon her astounded sense. And when he came she felt the singularly rapturous feeling that in her eyes he was a demi-god, that he perfected himself in her imagination, that everything in him was good. Now that he sat there before her, she saw him for the first time, and she saw that he was physically beautiful. The strength of his body was exalted into the strength of a young god, broad, and yet slender, sinewed as with the marble sinews of a statue; all this seeming so strange beneath the modernness of his frock coat. She saw his face completely for the first time. The cut of it was Roman, the head that of a Roman emperor, with its sensual profile, its small full mouth, living red under the brown gold of his curled mustachios. The forehead was low, the hair cut very close, like an enveloping black casque, and over that forehead, with its one line, hovered sadness, like a mist of age, strangely contradicting the wanton youthfulness of mouth and chin. And then his eyes, which she already knew, his eyes of mystery, small and deep set, with the deeper depth of their pupils, which seemed now to veil themselves and then again to look out.

But strangest was, that from all his beauty,
from all his being, from all his attitude, with his
hands folded between his knees, there came out
to her a magnetism which dominated her, draw-
ing her irresistibly towards him ; as if she had
suddenly, from the first moment of her self-
revelation, become *his*, to serve him in all things.
She felt this magnetism attracting her so violently
that every power in her melted into heaviness
and weakness. A weakness as if he might take
her and carry her away, anywhere, wherever he
wished ; a weakness as if she no longer possessed
her own thoughts, as if she had become nothing
—apart from him.

She felt this intensely ; and then, then came
the very strangest of all, when he continued
to sit there, at a respectful distance, his eyes
bearing a respectful look, his voice falling in
respectful accents. That was the very strangest

of all, that she saw him beneath her, while she felt him above her; that she wished to be his inferior, and he seemed to consider her higher than himself. She did not know how suddenly she so intensely realised this, but she did realise it, and it was the first pain love gave her.

"You are kind not to be angry with me," he began.

There was often something caressing in his voice; it was not clear, and now and then even a little broken, but this just gave it a certain charm of quality.

"Why?" she asked.

"In the first place I did wrong to pay you that visit. Secondly, I was ill-mannered at Mrs. Hoze's dinner."

"A whole catalogue of sins!" she laughed.

"Surely!" he continued, "and you are very good to bear me no malice."

" Perhaps that is because I always hear so much that is good about you at Dolf's."

" Have you never noticed anything odd in Dolf ? " he asked.

" No ; what do you mean ? "

" Has it never struck you that he has more of an eye for the great combinations of political questions than for the details of his own surroundings ? "

She looked at him, smiling, astonished.

" Yes," she said. " You are right. You know him well."

" Oh, we have known one another from boyhood. It is curious; he never sees the things that lie close to his hand ; he does not penetrate them. He is intellectually far-sighted."

" Yes," she assented.

" He does not know his wife, nor his daughters, nor Jules. He does not see what they have in

them. He identifies each of them by means of
a cypher fixed in his mind, which he forms out
of the two most prominent traits of character,
generally a little opposed. Mrs. van Attema
seems to him to have a heart of gold, but to be
not very practical : so much for her. Jules : a
musical genius, but an untractable boy : settled."

" Yes, he does not go very deeply into character," she said. " For there is a great deal
more in Amélie. . . ."

" And he is quite at sea about Jules," said
Quaerts. " Jules is thoroughly tractable, and
anything but a genius. Jules is nothing more
than an exceedingly receptive boy, with a little
rudimentary talent. And you . . . . he miscon-
ceives you, too ! "

" Me ? "

" Entirely ! Do you know what he thinks of
you ? "

" No."

" He thinks you—let me begin by telling you this—very, very sympathetic, and a dear little mother to your boys. But he thinks also that you are incapable of growing very fond of any one ; he thinks you a woman without passion, and melancholy for no reason, except for weariness. He thinks you weary yourself ! "

She looked at him quite alarmed, and saw him laughing mischievously.

" Never in my life am I weary ! " she said, and laughed, too, with full conviction.

" Of course not ! " he replied.

" How can *you* know ? " she asked.

" I feel it ! " he answered. " And, what is more, I know that the base of your character is not melancholy, not dark, but enthusiasm and light."

" I am not so sure of that myself," she scarcely

murmured, heavy, with that weakness within her; happy, that he should estimate her so exactly. "And do you, too," she continued, very airily, "think I am incapable of loving any one very much?"

"Now that is a matter of which I am not competent to judge," he said, with such frankness that his whole countenance suddenly grew younger, and the crease disappeared from his forehead. "I cannot tell that!"

" You seem to know a great deal about me otherwise," she laughed.

" I have seen you so often already."

" Barely four times."

" That is often."

She laughed brightly.

" Is that a compliment?"

" It is meant for one," he replied. " You do not know how much it means to me to see you."

How much it meant to him to see her! And
she felt herself so small, so weak, and him so
great, so perfect. With what decision he spoke,
how certain he seemed of it all! It almost
saddened her that it meant so much to him to
see her a single time. He placed her too high;
she did not wish to be placed so high.

And that delicate fragile something hung
between them again, as it had hung between
them at the dinner. Then it had been broken
by one ill-chosen word. Oh, that it might not
be broken now!"

"And now let us talk about *you*!" she said,
with affected frivolousness. "Do you know that
you take all sorts of pains to penetrate me, and that
I know nothing of you? That cannot be fair."

"If you knew how much I have given you
already! I give myself to you entirely; from
others I always conceal myself."

" Why ? "

" Because I am afraid of the others ! "

" *You* afraid ? "

" Yes. You think that I do not look as if I could feel afraid ? I have something. . . ."

He hesitated.

" Well ? " she asked.

" I have something that is very dear to me, and about which I am very anxious, lest any should touch it."

" And that is ? "

" My soul. I am not afraid of your touching it, for you would not hurt it. On the contrary, I know that it is very safe with you."

She would have liked once more, mechanically, to reproach him with his strangeness : she could not. But he guessed her thoughts.

" You think me a very odd person, do you not ? But how can I be otherwise with you ? "

She felt her love expanding within her heart, widening it to its full capacity within her. Her love was as a domain, in which he wandered.

"I do not understand you yet; I do not know you yet!" she said softly. "I do not see you yet. . . ."

"Would you be in any way interested to know me, to see me?"

"Surely."

"Let me tell you then; I should like to do so, it would be a great joy to me."

"I am listening to you most attentively."

"One question beforehand: You cannot endure an athlete?"

"On the contrary, I do not mind the display and development of strength so long as it is not too near me. Just as I like to hear a storm, when I am safely within doors. And I can look at acrobats with great pleasure."

He laughed quietly.

"Nevertheless you held my particular pre-dilection in great aversion?"

"Why should you think that?"

"I felt it."

"You feel everything," she said, almost in alarm. "You are a dangerous person."

"So many think that. Shall I tell you why you took a special aversion in my case?"

"Yes."

"Because you did not understand it in me; even though you may perhaps have observed that physical exercise is one of my strong passions."

"I do not understand you at all."

"I think you are right . . . . But do not let me talk so much of myself; I prefer to talk of you."

"And I of you. So be gallant to me for the first time in our acquaintance, and speak . . . . of yourself."

He bowed, with a smile.

" You will not think me tiresome ? "

" Not at all.   You were telling me of yourself. You were speaking of your love of exercise . . . . "

" Ah! yes . . . . Can you understand that there are in me two distinct individuals ? "

" Two distinct . . . . "

" Yes.   My soul, my real self; and then . . . . there remains the other."

" And what is that other ? "

" Something ugly, something common, something grossly primitive.   In one word, the brute."

She shrugged her shoulders lightly.

" How dark you paint yourself.   The same thing is more or less true of everybody."

" Yes, but it troubles me more than I can tell you.   I suffer; the lower hurts my soul, the higher, more than the whole world hurts it. Now do you know why I feel such a sense of

security when I am with you? It is because I
do not feel the brute that is in me. . . . Let me
go on a little longer, let me shrive myself; it does
me good to tell you all this. You thought I had
only seen you four times? But I saw you so
often formerly, in the theatre, in the street,
everywhere. There was always something strange
for me when I saw you in the midst of accidental
surroundings. And always, when I looked at you,
I felt as if I were lifted to something more
beautiful. I cannot express myself more clearly.
There is something in your face, in your eyes,
in your movements, I do not know what, but
something better than in other people, something
that addressed itself, most eloquently, to my soul
only. All this is so subtle and so strange . . . .
But you are no doubt thinking again that I am
going too far, are you not? Or that I am
raving?"

" Certainly, I never should have thought you such an idealist, such a *sensitivist,*" said Cecile softly.

" Have I leave to speak to you like this ? "

" Why not ? " she asked, to escape the necessity of replying directly.

" You might possibly fear lest I should compromise you. . . . "

" I do not fear that for an instant ! " she replied, haughtily, as in utter contempt of the world.

They were silent a moment. That delicate fragile thing, that might so easily break, still hung between them, thin, like a gossamer, lightly joining them together. An atmosphere of embarrassment hovered about them. They felt that the words which had passed between them were full of significance. Cecile waited for him to continue ; but as he was silent she boldly took up the conversation :

"On the contrary, I value it highly that you have spoken to me like this. You were right; you have indeed given me much of yourself. I wish to assure you of my sympathy. I believe I understand you better now that I see you better."

"I want very much to ask you something," he said, "but I dare not."

She smiled to encourage him.

"No, really I dare not," he repeated.

"Shall I guess?" Cecile asked, jestingly.

"Yes; what do you think it is?"

She glanced round the room until her eye rested on the little table covered with books.

"The loan of Emerson's Essays?" she hazarded.

But Quaerts shook his head and laughed.

"No, thank you," he said. "I have bought the volume long ago. No, no; it is a much greater favour than the loan of a book."

" Be bold then, and ask it," Cecile went on, still jestingly.

" I dare not," he said again. " I should not know how to put my request into words."

She looked at him earnestly, into his eyes, gazing steadily upon her, and then she said :

" I know what you want to ask me, but I will not say it. *You* must do that : so seek your words."

" If you know, will you permit me then to say it ? "

" Yes, for if my surmise is correct, it is nothing that you may not ask."

" And yet it would be a great favour . . . . But let me warn you beforehand that I look upon myself as some one of a much lower order than you."

A shadow passed across her face, her mouth had a little contraction of pain, and she pressed him, a little unnerved :

"I beg you, ask. Just ask me simply."

"It is a wish, then, that sympathy were sealed between you and me. Would you allow me to come to you when I am unhappy? I always feel so happy in your presence, so soothed, so different from the state of ordinary life, for with you I live only my better, my true self—you know what I mean."

Everything melted again within her into weakness and heaviness; he placed her upon too high a pedestal; she was happy, because of what he asked her, but sad, that he felt himself less than she.

"Very well," she said, nevertheless, with a clear voice. "It is as you wish."

And she gave him her hand, her beautiful, long, white hand, where on one white finger gleamed the sparks of jewels, white and blue. A moment, very reverently, he pressed her finger-tips between his own.

" Thank you," he said in a hushed voice, a voice that was a little broken.

" Are you often unhappy ? " asked Cecile.

" Always . . . ." he replied, almost humbly, and as though embarrassed at having to confess it. " I do not know what it means, only that it has always been so. And yet from my childhood I have enjoyed much that people call happiness. But yet, yet . . . . I suffer through myself. It is I who do myself the most hurt. And after that the world . . . . and I must always hide myself. To the world I only show the individual who rides and fences and hunts, who goes into society and is dangerous for young married women . . . ."

He laughed with his bad low laugh, looking aslant into her eyes ; she remained calmly gazing at him.

" Beyond that I give them nothing. I hate

them ; I have nothing in common with them, thank God ! "

" You are too proud," said Cecile. " Each of those people has his own sorrow, just as you have ; the one suffers a little more subtly, the other a little more coarsely ; but they all suffer. And in that they all resemble yourself."

" Each taken by himself, perhaps ! But that is not how I take them ; I take them in the lump, and I hate them. Do not you ? "

" No," she said calmly. " I do not believe I am capable of hating."

" You are strong within yourself. You suffice to yourself."

" No, no, not that, really not ; but you .... you are unjust towards the world."

" Possibly : why does it always give me pain ? Alone with you I forget that it exists, the outside world. Do you understand now why I was

9

so sorry to see you at Mrs. Hoze's? You seemed
to me to have lowered yourself. And it was
because . . . . because of this peculiarity I saw in
you that I did not seek your acquaintance earlier.
This acquaintance was fatally bound to come, and
so I waited . . . ."

Fate, what would it bring her? thought Cecile.
But she could not think deeply; she seemed to
herself to be dreaming of beautiful and subtle
things which did not exist for other people,
which only floated between them two. There
was no longer need to look upon them as illusions, it was as if she had overtaken the future!
One short moment only did this endure as
happiness; then again she felt pain, on account
of his reverence.

VI.

He was gone and she was alone, waiting for
the children. She neglected to ring for the

lamp to be lighted, and the twilight of the late afternoon darkened in the room. She sat motionless, and looked out before her at the withered trees.

"Why should I not be happy?" she thought. "He is happy with me; he is himself with me only; he cannot be so among other people. Why then can *I* not be happy?"

She felt pain; her soul suffered, it seemed to her for the first time. This, perhaps, was because now for the first time her soul had not been itself but another. It seemed to her that another woman must have spoken to him, to Quaerts, just now. An exalted woman: a woman of illusions—the woman, in fact, he saw in her, and not the woman she was: lowly, a woman of love. Ah, she had had to restrain herself not to ask him: "Why do you speak to me like that? Why do you raise up your beautiful thoughts to

me? Why do you not rather let them drip
down upon me? For see, I do not stand so
high as you think; and see, I am at your feet,
and my eyes seek you above me."

Should she have told him that she deceived
him? Should she have asked him: "How is it
that I lower myself when I mix with other
people? What then do you see in me? I am
only a woman, a woman of feebleness and dreams.
I have come to love you, I do not know why."
Should she have opened his eyes and said to him:
"Look upon your own soul in a mirror; look
upon yourself and see how you are a god walking
upon the earth: a god who knows everything
because he feels it, feels it because he knows
it. . . ." Everything? . . . . No . . . . not everything; for he deceived himself, this god, and
thought to find an equal in her, who was but his
creature. Should she have declared all this, at

the cost of her modesty and his happiness?
For his happiness—she felt perfectly assured
—lay in seeing her in the way that he saw
her.

" With me he is happy ! " she thought. " And
sympathy is sealed between us. . . . It was not
friendship, nor did he speak of love; he called
it simply sympathy. . . . With me he feels only
his real self, and not that other . . . . the brute
that is in him . . . . the brute. . . . "

Then there came drifting over her a gloom as
of gathering clouds, and she shuddered before
that which suddenly rolled through her : a
broad stream of blackness, as though its waters
were filled with mud, which bubbled up in
troubled rings, growing larger and larger. She
took fear before this stream, and tried not to
see it; but it sullied all her landscapes so
bright before, with their horizons of light—

now with a sky of ink smeared above, like filthy night.

" How high he thinks, how noble his thoughts are ! " Cecile still forced herself to imagine, in spite of . . . .

But the magic was gone : her admiration of his lofty thoughts tumbled away into an abyss; then suddenly, by a lightning flash through the night of that inken sky, she saw clearly that his exalted intellect was a supreme sorrow to her.

It had become quite dark in the room. Cecile, afraid of the lightning which revealed her to herself, fell back upon the cushions of the settee. She hid her face in her hands, pressing her eyes, as though she wished, after this moment of self-revelation, to be blind for ever.

But demoniacally it raged through her, a hurricane of hell, a storm of passion, which blew up out of the darkness of the landscape, lashing up the tossed waves of the foul stream toward the sky of ink.

"Oh!" she moaned. " I am unworthy of him . . . . unworthy. . . ."

CHAPTER III.

I.

QUAERTS lived on the Plein, above a tailor, where he occupied two small rooms, furnished in the most ordinary style. He might have lived far better, but he was indifferent to comfort; he never gave it a thought in his own place; when he came across it elsewhere it did not attract him. But it troubled Jules that Quaerts should live in this fashion, and the boy had long wished to embellish his rooms. He was busy at this moment hanging some trophies on an armour-rack, standing on a pair of steps, humming a tune he remembered from an opera. Quaerts gave no heed to what Jules was doing; he lay immobile on the sofa, at full length, in his flannel, unshorn, his eyes fixed upon the florid decoration of the Palace of Justice, tracing a background of architecture behind the withered trees of the Plein.

" Look, Taco, will this do ? " asked Jules, after hanging an Algerian sabre between two creeses, and draping the folds of a Javanese sarong between.

" Beautifully," answered Quaerts. But he did not look at the trophies, and continued gazing at the Palace. He lay motionless. There was no thought in him; only listless dissatisfaction with himself, and consequent sadness. For three weeks he had led a life of debauch, to deaden consciousness, or perhaps he did not know precisely what : something that was in him, something that was fine, but tiresome in ordinary life. He had begun with shooting, in North Brabant, over a friend's land. It lasted a week; there were eight of

them; sport in the open air, followed by sporting
dinners, with not only a great deal of wine,
certainly the best, but still more geneva, also very
fine, like a liqueur. Turbulent excursions on
horseback in the neighbourhood; madnesses perpe-
trated at a farm—the peasant-woman carried round
in a barrel, and locked up in the cowhouse—
mischievous exploits worthy only of unruly boys
and savages; at the end of it all, in a police-court,
a summons, with a fine and damages. Wound up
to a pitch of excitement with too much sport, too
much oxygen, and too much wine, five of the
pack, among whom was Quaerts, had gone on to
Brussels. There they had stayed almost a fortnight, leading a life of continual excess—champagne and larking; a wild joy of living, which,
natural enough at first, has in the end to be
screwed up and screwed up higher still, to make
it last a couple of days longer; the last nights

spent weariedly over *écarté*, with none but the fixed idea of winning, the exhaustion of all their violence already pulsing through their bodies, like nervous relaxation, their eyes gazing without expression upon the cards of the game.

During that time Quaerts had only once thought of Cecile; and he had not followed up the thought. She had no doubt arisen three or four times in his brain, a vague image, white and transparent; an apparition which had vanished again immediately, leaving no trace of its passage. All this time too he had not written to her, and it had only once struck him that a silence of three weeks, after their last conversation, must at least seem strange to her. There it had remained. He was back now; he had lain three days long at home on his bed, on his sofa, tired, feverish, dissatisfied, disgusted with everything, everything; then one morning, remembering that it was Wednesday, he had thought of Jules and his riding-lesson.

He sent for Jules, but too lazy to shave or dress, he remained lying where he was. And he still lay there, realising nothing. There before him was the Palace. Next to it the Privy Council. At the side he could see the White Club, and William the Silent standing on his pedestal in the middle of the Plein : that was all exceedingly interesting. And Jules was hanging up trophies : also interesting. And the most interesting of all was the stupid life he had been leading. What tension to give the lie to his ennui ! Had he really amused himself during that time ? No ; he had made a pretence of being amused : the peasant-woman episode and the *écart!* ; the sport had been bad ; the wine good, but he had drunk too much of it. And then that particularly filthy champagne .... at Brussels. . . . And

what then? He had absolute need of it, of a
life like that, of sport and wild enjoyment; it
served to balance the other thing that was in
him, that was tiresome for him in ordinary life.

But why was it not possible to preserve some
mean, in one as well as in the other? He was
well equipped for ordinary life, and with that
he possessed something in addition; why could
he not remain balanced between those two
spheres of disposition? Why was he always
tossed from one to the other, as a thing be-
longing to neither? How fine he could have
made his life with only the least tact, the least
self-restraint! How he might have lived in a
healthy joy of purified animal existence, tem-
pered by a higher joyousness of soul! But tact,
self-restraint—he had none of these; he lived
according to his impulses, always in extremes;
he was incapable of half indulgences. And in

this lay his pride as well as his regret ; his pride that he felt " wholly " whatever he felt, that he was unable to make terms with his emotions ; and his regret, that he could *not* make terms and bring into harmony the elements which warred for ever within him.

When he had met Cecile, and had seen her again, and yet once more, he had felt himself carried wholly to the one extremity, the summit of exaltation, of pure crystal sympathy, in which the circle of his atmosphere—as he had said— glided over hers, a caress of pure chastity and spirituality, as two stars, spinning closer to- gether, might mingle their atmospheres for a moment, like breaths. What smiling happiness had been within his reach, as a grace from Heaven !

Then, then, he had felt himself toppling down, as if he had rocked over the balancing-point ; and

he had longed for the earthly, for great simplicity of emotion, for primitive enjoyment of
life, for flesh and blood. He remembered now
how, two days after his last conversation with
Cecile, he had seen Emilie Hijdrecht, here in his
rooms, where at length, stung by his neglect, she
had ventured to come to see him one evening,
heedless of all caution. With a line of cruelty
round his mouth he recalled how she had wept
at his knees, how in her jealousy she had com-
plained against Cecile, how he had bidden her
be silent, and not pronounce Cecile's name.
Then, their mad embrace, an embrace of cruelty :
cruelty on her part against the man whom time
after time she lost when she thought him secured
for good and all, whom she could not understand,
to whom she clung with all the violence of her
brutal passion, a purely animal passion of primitive times ; cruelty on his part against the woman

he despised, while in his passion he almost stifled her in his embrace.

II.

And what then? How to find the mean between the two poles of his nature. He shrugged his shoulders. He knew he could never find it. He lacked some quality, or a certain power, necessary to find it. He could do nothing but allow himself to swing to and fro. Very well then : he would let himself swing. There was nothing else to do. For now, in the lassitude following his outburst of savagery, he began to experience again an ardent longing, like some one who, after a long evening passed in a ball-room, heavy with foul air of gaslight and a stifling crush and oppression of human breath, craves a high heaven and width of atmosphere ; a passionate longing towards Cecile. And he smiled, glad that he knew her, that he was able to go to her, that

it was his privilege to enter into the chaste
inclosure of her sanctity, as into a temple; he
smiled, glad that he felt this longing, and proud,
exalting himself above all other men. Already
he tasted the pleasure of confessing to her how
he had lived during the last three weeks; and
already he heard her voice, although he could
not distinguish the words . . . .

Jules descended from the ladder. He was
disappointed that Quaerts had not followed his
arrangement of the weapons upon the rack, and
his drapery of the stuffs around them. But he
had quietly continued his work, and now that it
was finished, he came down and went quietly to
sit upon the floor, with his head against the
foot of the sofa where his friend lay thinking.
Jules said never a word; he looked straight
before him, a little sulkily, knowing that Quaerts
was looking at him.

10

" Jules ! " said Quaerts.

But Jules did not answer, still staring.

" Tell me, Jules ! Why do you like me so much ? "

" How should I know ? " answered Jules, with thin lips.

" Don't you know ? "

" No. How can you know why you are fond of any one ? "

" You ought not to be so fond of me, Jules. It's not good."

" Very well, I will be less so in the future."

Jules rose suddenly, and took his hat. He held out his hand, but, laughing, Quaerts held him.

" You see, scarcely any one is fond of me, save .... you and your father. Now I know why your father is fond of me, but not why you are."

" You are always wanting to know something."

" Is that so very wrong ? "

" Certainly. You will never be satisfied. Mamma always says that no one knows anything."

" And you ? "

" I . . . . nothing . . . ."

" What do you mean . . . . nothing ? "

" I know nothing at all . . . . Let me go."

" Are you cross, Jules ? "

" No; but I have an engagement."

" Can't you wait until I have dressed, then we can go together ? I am going to Aunt Cecile's."

Jules objected.

" Very well, only hurry."

Quaerts rose up. He now saw the arrangement of the weapons, about which he had quite forgotten : " You have done it very prettily, Jules," he said, admiringly. " Thank you very much."

Jules did not answer, and Quaerts went through into his dressing-room. The lad sat down on the sofa, bolt upright, looking out upon the Palace, across the bareness of the withered trees. His eyes filled with great round tears, which fell down. Still and motionless, he wept.

III.

Cecile had passed those same three weeks in a state of ignorance which had filled her with pain. Through Dolf she had indeed heard that Quaerts was away shooting, but beyond that nothing. A thrill of joy electrified her when the door behind the screen opened, and she saw him enter the room. He stood before her before she could recover herself, and as she was trembling she did not rise up, but still sitting, reached out her hand to him, her fingers quivering imperceptibly.

" I have been out of town," he began.

" So I heard . . . ."

" Have you been well all this time ? "

" Quite well, thank you."

He noticed she was somewhat pale, that she had a light blue shadow under her eyes, and that there was lassitude in all her movements. But he thought there was nothing extraordinary in that, or that perhaps she seemed pale in the cream colour of her soft white dress, like silken wool, even as her form was yet slighter in the constraint of the scarf about her waist, with its long white fringe falling to her feet. She sat alone with Christie, the child upon his footstool with his head in her lap, a picture-book upon his knees.

" You two are a perfect Madonna and Child," said Quaerts.

" Little Dolf is gone out to walk with his

godfather," she said, looking fondly upon her child, and gently motioning to him.

At which bidding the little boy stood up and shyly approached Quaerts, offering him a tiny hand. Quaerts took him up and set him upon his knee.

" How light he is ! "

" He is not strong," said Cecile.

" You codle him too much."

She laughed.

" Pedagogue ! " she said, bantering. " How do I codle him ? "

" I always find him nestling against your skirts. He must come with me one of these days. You should let him try some gymnastics."

" Jules horse-riding and Christie gymnastics ! " she exclaimed.

" Yes . . . . sport in fact," he answered, with a look of malice.

She looked back at him, and sympathy smiled from the depths of her gold-grey eyes. He felt thoroughly happy, and with the child still upon his knees he said:

" I come to confess to you . . . . Lady ! "

Then, as though startled, he put the child away from him.

" To confess ? "

" Yes . . . . Christie, go back to mamma; I must not keep you by me any longer."

" Very well," said Christie, with great wondering eyes.

" The child would forgive too easily," said Quaerts.

" And I, have I anything to forgive you ? " she asked.

" I shall be only too happy if you will see it in that light."

" Begin then."

" *Le petit Jésus* . . . ." he hesitated.

Cecile stood up; she took the child, kissed him, and sat him on a stool by the window with his picture-book. Then she came back to the *chaise-longue.*

" He will not hear . . . ."

And Quaerts began the story, choosing his words; he spoke of the shooting, the escapades, the peasant-woman, and of Brussels. She listened attentively, with dread in her eyes at the violence of such a life, the echo of which reverberated in his words, even though the echo was softened by his reverence.

" And is all this a sinfulness needing absolution ? " she asked, when it was finished.

" Is it not ? "

" I am no madonna, but . . . . a woman whose ideas have been somewhat emancipated. If you were happy in what you did it was no sin, for

happiness is good . . . . Were you happy then,
I ask you ? For in that case what you did
was . . . . good."

" Happy ? " he asked.

" Yes."

" No . . . . therefore I have sinned, sinned
against myself, have I not ? Forgive me . . . .
Lady."

She was troubled at the sound of his voice,
which, caressively broken, wrapped her about in a
charm ; she was troubled to see him sitting
there, filling with his personality a place in her
room beside her. In one second she lived
whole hours, feeling her calm love heavy within
her, a not oppressive weight, feeling a longing
to throw her arms about him and tell him
that she worshipped him ; feeling also fervent
sorrow at what he had confessed : that again
he had been unhappy. Hardly able to

control herself in her compassion, she stood up,
stepped towards him, and laid her hand upon his
shoulder :

" Tell me, do you mean all this?   Is it all
true?   Is it true that you have lived as you say,
and yet have not been happy ? "

" Perfectly true, on my soul."

" Then why did you do it ? "

" I could not do otherwise."

" You were unable to force yourself to moder-
ation ? "

" Absolutely."

" Then I should like to teach you."

" And I should not like to learn, from *you.*
For it is and always will be my best happiness
to be immoderate also where you are concerned ;
excessive in the emotion of my secret self, my
soul, just as I have now been excessive in the
grossness of my evident self."

Her eyes grew dim, she shook her head, her hand still upon his shoulder.

"That is not right," she said, deeply distressed.

" It is a joy . . . . for both those beings. I must be so . . . . I cannot but be immoderate . . . . both demand it."

" But that is not right," she insisted. " Pure enjoyment. . . ."

" The lowest, but also the highest. . . ."

A shiver passed through her, a deadly fear for him.

" No, no," she persisted. " Do not think that. Do not do it. Neither the one nor the other. Really, it is all wrong. Pure joy, unbridled joy, even the highest, is not good. In that way you force your life. When you speak so I am afraid for your sake. Try to recover some balance. You have so many possibilities of being happy."

" Oh, yes. . . ."

" Yes; but what I mean is, do not be fanatical. And . . . . and also, for the love of God, do not again run so madly after pleasure."

He looked up at her, he saw her beseeching him with her eyes, with the expression of her face, with her whole attitude as she stood bending slightly forward. He *saw* her beseeching him, as he *heard* her, and then he knew that she loved him. A feeling of bright rapture came upon him, as if something high descended upon him to guide him. He did not stir—he felt her hand thrilling at his shoulder—afraid, lest with the smallest movement he should drive that rapture away. It did not occur to him for a moment to speak a word of tenderness to her, or to take her in his arms and press her to him; she was so transfigured in his eyes that any such profane desire remained far away from him.

Yet he felt at that moment that he loved her;
but as he had never yet loved any before; so
completely and exclusively, with the noblest that
is hidden away in the soul, often unknown even
to itself. He felt that he loved her with new-
born feelings of frank youth and fresh vigour,
and pure unselfishness. And it seemed to him
that it was all a dream of something which did
not exist, a dream lightly woven about him, a
web of sunbeams.

" Lady !" he whispered. " Forgive me. . . ."

" Promise then. . . ."

" Willingly, but I shall not be able to keep my
promise. I am weak. . . ."

" No."

" Ah, I am. But I give my promise, and I
promise also to try my utmost to keep it. Will
you forgive me now ? "

She nodded to him; her smile fell on him like

a burst of sunlight. Then she went to the child,
took him in her arms, and brought him to
Quaerts :

" Put your arms round his neck, Christie, and
give him a kiss."

He took the child from her; he threw his little
arms about his neck, and kissed him on the
forehead.

" *Le petit Jésus !* " he whispered.

IV.

They stayed long talking to one another, and
no one came to disturb them. The child had
gone back to sit by the window. Twilight began
to strew pale ashes in the room. He saw Cecile
sitting there, sweetly white; the melody of her
half-breathed words came rippling towards him
benignly. They talked of many things: of
Emerson ; Van Eeden's new poem in the *Nieuwe
Gids*; views of life. He accepted a cup of tea

only for the pleasure of seeing her move with the febrile lines of her graciousness, standing before the tea table in the corner. In her white dress there was something about her of marble grown lissom with inspiration and warm life. He sat motionless, listening reverently, swathed in a still rapture of delight; a mood which defied analysis, without a visible origin, springing from their sympathetic fellowship as a flower springs from an invisible seed after a drop of rain and a kiss of the sunshine. She too was happy; she no longer felt the pain his reverence had caused her. True she was a little sad by reason of what he had told her, but she was happy for the sake of the speck of the present. Nor longer did she see that dark stream, that inken sky, that night landscape; everything now was light and calm, and happiness breathed about her, tangible, a living caress. Sometimes they ceased speaking

and looked towards the child, reading; or he
would ask them something and they would
answer. Then they smiled one to another,
because the child was so good and did not disturb
them.

" If only this could continue for ever," he
ventured to say, though still fearing lest a word
might break the crystalline transparency of their
happiness. " If you could only see into me now,
how all in me is peace. I do not know why, but
so it is. Perhaps because of your forgiveness.
Forgiveness is a thing so dear to people of weak
character.

" But I cannot think your character weak. It
is not. You tell me you know sometimes how
to place yourself above ordinary life, whence you
can look down upon its griefs as on a comedy
which makes one laugh sadly for a minute, but
which is not true. I too believe that life as we

see it is only a symbol of a true life concealed beneath it, which we do not see. But I cannot, for
my part, rise beyond the symbol, while you can.
Therefore you are strong and know yourself great."

" How strange, when I just think myself weak,
and you great and powerful. You dare to be
what you are, in all your harmony; I always hide,
and am afraid of people individually, though.
sometimes I am able to rise above life in the
mass. But these are riddles which it is vain for
me to attempt to solve, and though I have not
the power to solve them, at this moment I feel
nothing but happiness. Surely I may say that
once, audibly, may I not—audibly? "

She smiled to him in the blessedness of making
him happy.

" It is the first time I have felt happy in this
way," he continued. " Indeed it is the first time
I have felt happy at all. . . ."

11

" Then do not analyse it."

"There is no need. It is standing before me
in all its simplicity. Do you know why I am
happy ? "

" Do not analyse it. . . ." she repeated,
frightened.

" No," he said, " but may I tell you, without
analysis ? "

"No, do not," she stammered, " because . . . .
because I know. . . ."

She besought him, very pale, with folded
trembling hands. The child looked at them ; he
had closed his book, and come to sit down on
his stool by his mother, with a look of merry
sagacity in his pale blue eyes.

" Then I obey you," said Quaerts, with some
difficulty.

And they were both silent, their eyes expanded
as with the lustre of a vision. It seemed to be

gently beaming about them, through the pale
ashen twilight.

V.

This evening Cecile had written a great deal
into her diary, and now she paced up and down
in her room, with locked hands hanging down,
her head slightly bowed, and with a fixed look.
There was anxiety about her mouth. Before her
was the vision, as she had conceived it. He
loved her with his soul alone, not as a woman
who is pretty and good ; with a higher love than
that, with the finest fibre of his being—his real
being—with supreme emotion of the very essence
of his deepest soul. Thus she felt that he had
loved her and no other way, with contemplation,
with adoration. Thus she felt it in truth through
that identity of sympathy by which each of them
knew what passed within the other. And that
was his happiness—his first, as he said—thus

to love her, and no other wise. Oh, she well
understood him. She understood his illusion,
what he saw in her; and now she knew that, if
she really wished to love him for his, and not for
her own sake, she must seem no other before
him, she must preserve his illusion of a woman
not of flesh, who desired nothing of the earth,
as other women were to him; who should be soul
alone; a sister soul to his. But while she saw
before her this vision of her love, calm and
radiant, she saw also the struggle which awaited
her; the struggle with herself, with her own
distress: distress that he thought upon her so
highly, and named her madonna, the while she
longed only to be lowly and his slave. She would
have to seem the woman he saw in her, for the
sake of his happiness, and the part would be a
heavy one for her to support, for she loved him,
ah ! with such simplicity, with all her woman's

heart, wishing to give herself to him entirely, as only once in her life a woman gives herself, whatever the sacrifice might cost her, the sacrifice made in ignorance of herself, and perhaps later to be made in bitterness and sorrow. The outward appearance of her conduct and her inward consciousness of herself; the conflict of these would fall heavily upon her, but she thought upon the struggle with a smile, with joy beaming through her heart, for this bitterness would be endured for *him*, deliberately for him, alone for him. Oh, the luxury to suffer for one loved as she loved him; to be tortured with longing within oneself, that he might not come to her with the embrace of his arms and the kiss of his mouth; and to feel that the torture was for the sake of his happiness, his! To feel that she loved him sufficiently to go to him with wide arms and beg for alms of his caresses; but also to feel that she

had more love for him than that, and higher,
and that—not out of pride or bashfulness, which
are really egoism, but solely from sacrifice of
herself to his happiness—she never would, never
could, be a suppliant in that sense.

To suffer, to suffer for him! To wear a sword
through her soul for him! To be a martyr for
her god, for whom there was no happiness save
through her martyrdom! And she had passed
her life, long, long years, without having felt
until this day that such luxury could exist, not
as fantasy in rhymes, but as reality in her heart.
She had been a young girl, and had read the
poets and what they rhyme of love, and she had
thought she understood it all, with a subtle comprehension; yet without ever having had the
least acquaintance with the emotion itself. She
had been a young woman, had been married, had
borne children. Her married life dashed through

her mind in a lightning-flash of memory, and she
stopped still before the portrait of her dead
husband, standing there on its easel, draped in
sombre plush. The mask it wore was of ambition : an austere, refined face, with features
sharp, as if engraved in fine steel; coldly intelligent eyes with a fixed portrait look ; thin, clean-
shaven lips, closed firmly like a lock. Her
husband ! And she still lived in the same house
where she had lived with him, where she had had
to receive her many guests when he was Foreign
Minister. Her receptions and dinners flickered
up in her mind, scenes of worldliness, and she
clearly recalled her husband's eye taking in
everything with a quick glance of approval or
condemnation : the arrangement of her rooms,
her dress, the ordering of her parties. Her
marriage had not been an unhappy one; her
husband was a little cold and unexpansive,

wrapped wholly in his ambition, but he was attached to her after his fashion, even with tenderness; she too had been fond of him; she thought at the time that she was marrying him for love: her dependent womanliness loving the male, the master. Of a delicate constitution, probably undermined by excessive brain-work, he had died after a short illness. Cecile remembered her sorrow, her loneliness with the two children, about whom he had already feared lest she should spoil them. And her loneliness had been sweet to her, among the clouds of her dreaming. . . .

This portrait—a costly life-size photograph; a carbon impression dark with a Rembrandt shadow —why had she never had it copied in oils, as she had at first intended? The intention had died down of itself; for months she had not thought of the matter, now suddenly it recurred to her. . . .

And she felt no self-reproach or remorse. She would not now have it done. It was well enough as it was. She thought of the dead man without sorrow. She had never had cause to complain of him; he had never had anything with which to reproach her. And now she was free; she became conscious of the fact with exultation. Free to feel what she would. Her freedom arched above her as a blue firmament in which new love ascended with a dove's immaculate flight. Freedom, air, light! She turned away from the portrait with a smile of rapture; she thrust her arms above her head as if she would measure her freedom, the width of the air, as if she would go to meet the light. Love, she was in love! There was nothing but love; nothing but the harmony of their souls, the harmony of her handmaiden's soul with the soul of her god, an exile upon the earth. Oh, how blessed that this harmony could exist between him so exalted and her so lowly! But he must not see her lowliness; she must remain the madonna, for his sake, in the martyrdom of his reverence, in the dizziness of the high place to which he raised her, beside himself. She felt this dizziness shuddering about her like rings of light. She threw herself upon her sofa, and locked her fingers; her eyelids quivered, and then she remained staring towards some very distant point.

VI.

Jules had been away from school for a day or two with a 'bad headache, which had made him look pale, and given him an air of sadness; but he was a little better now, and growing weary of his own room he went downstairs to the empty drawing-room, and sat at the piano. Papa was at work in his study, but it would not interfere

with papa if he played. Dolf spoilt him, seeing
something in his son that was wanting in himself
and that therefore attracted him, as this had
possibly formerly attracted him in his wife also ;
Jules could do no wrong in his eyes, and if the
boy had only been willing, Dolf would have
spared no expense to give him a careful musical
education. But Jules opposed himself violently
to anything in any way resembling lessons, and
maintained besides that it was not worth while.
He had no ambition ; his vanity was not tickled
by his father's hopes in him and appreciation of
his playing ; he played for himself only, to express
himself in the vague language of musical sounds.
At this moment he felt himself alone, abandoned
in the great house, though he knew that papa
was at work two rooms off, and that when he
pleased he could take refuge on papa's great
couch ; he felt within himself an almost physical

feeling of dread at his loneliness, which caused something to reel about him, an inward sense of inner desolation.

He was fourteen years old, but he felt himself neither child nor boy : a certain feebleness, a need almost feminine of dependency, of devotion to some one who would be everything to him, had already, in his earliest childhood, struck into his virility, and it shivered through him in his dread of this inner loneliness, as if he were afraid of himself. He suffered greatly from the vague moods in which that strange something oppressed him ; then, not knowing where to hide his inner being, he would go to play, so that he might lose himself in the great sound-soul of music. His thin, nervous fingers would grope querulously over the keys, and false chords would be struck in his search ; then he would let himself go, find some single motive, very short, of plaintive minor

melancholy, and caress that motive in his joy
at having found it, caress it until it returned
each moment as a monotony of sorrow, thinking
it so beautiful that he could not leave it. So
well did they sing all that he felt, those four or
five notes, that he would play them over and
over again, until Suzette would burst into the
room and make him stop lest she should be
driven mad.

Thus he played now. It was pitiful at first;
he barely recognised the notes; harsh discords
wailed up and cut into his poor brain, still
smarting from his headache. He moaned as if
he were in pain afresh; but his fingers were
hypnotised, they could not desist, they still
sought on, and the notes became purer; a short
phrase released itself with a cry, a cry which
continually returned on the same note, suddenly
high after the bass of the prelude. This note

came as a surprise to Jules; that fair cry of
sorrow frightened him, and he was glad to have
found it, glad to have so sweet a sorrow. Then
he was no longer himself; he played on until he
felt it was not himself who was playing, but
another within him who compelled him; he
found the full pure chords as by intuition;
through the sobbing of the sounds ran the same
musical figure, higher and higher, with silver
feet of purity, following the curve of crystal
rainbows lightly spanned on high; reaching the
topmost point of the crystal arch it struck a cry,
this time in very drunkenness, out into the
major, throwing up wide arms in gladness to
heavens of intangible blue. Then it was like
souls of men, which first live and suffer and utter
their complaint, and then die, to glitter in forms
of light whose long wings spring from their pure
shoulders in sheets of silver light; they trip one

behind the other over the rainbows, over the
bridges of glass, blue, and rose, and yellow; and
there come more and more, kindreds and nations
of souls; they hurry their silver feet, they press
across the rainbows, they laugh and sing and
push one another; in their jostling their wings
clash together, scattering silver down. Now
they stand all on the top of the arc, and look
up, with the great wondering of their laughing
child-eyes; and they dare not, they dare not, but
others press on behind them, innumerable, more
and more, and yet more; they crowd upwards
to the topmost height, their wings straight
in the air, close together. Now, now they must;
they may hesitate no longer. One of them, taking
deep breath, spreads his flight, and with one
shock springs out of the thick throng into the
ether. Soon many follow, and one after another,
till their shapes swoon in the blue; all is gleam

about them. Now, far below, thin as a thin thread, the rainbow arches itself, but they do not look at it; rays fall towards them—these are souls, which they embrace—they go with them in locked embraces. And then the light. Light beaming over all; all things liquid in everlasting light; nothing but light, the sounds sing the light, the sounds are the light, there is nothing now but the Light, everlasting. . . .

" Jules ! "

He looked up vacantly.

" Jules ! Jules ! "

He smiled now, as if awaked from a dream-sleep; he rose, went to her, to Cecile. She stood in the doorway; she had remained standing there while he played; it had seemed to her that he was playing a part of herself.

" What were you playing, Jules ? " she asked.

He was quite awake now, and distressed, fear-

ing he must have made a terrible noise in the
house. . . ."

" I don't know, auntie," he said.

She hugged him, suddenly, violently, in grati-
tude. . . . To him she owed It, the great Mystery,
since the day when he had broken out in anger
against her. . . .

CHAPTER IV.

I.

" On, for that which cannot be told, because words are so few, always the same, varying combinations of a few letters and sounds; oh, for that which cannot be thought of in the narrow limits of comprehension ; that which at best can only be groped for with the antennæ of the soul ; essence of the essences of the ultimate elements of our being. . . ."

She wrote no more, she knew no more : why write that she had no words, and still seek them ?

She was waiting for him, and she looked out of the open window to see if he came. She remained looking a long time ; then she felt that

178

he would come immediately, and so he did; she saw him approaching along the Scheveningen Road ; he pushed open the iron gate of the villa, and smiled to her as he raised his hat.

" Wait ! " she cried. " Stay where you are ! "

She ran down the steps, into the garden, where he stood. She came towards him, beaming with happiness, and so lovely, so delicately frail: her blonde head so seemly in the fresh green of May ; her figure—a young girl's—in the palest grey gown, with black velvet ribbon, and silver lace here and there.

" I am glad you have come. You have not been to see me for so long ! " she said, giving her hand.

He did not answer at once.

" Let us sit in the garden, behind, the weather is so fine."

" Let us," he said.

They walked into the garden, by the mesh of the garden paths, the jasmine vines starring white as they passed. In an adjoining villa a piano was playing; the sounds came to them of Rubinstein's Romance in Es.

" Listen ! " said Cecile, starting up. " What is that ? "

" What ? " he asked.

" What they are playing."

"Something of Rubinstein's, I believe," he replied.

" Rubinstein. . . . ? " she repeated, emptily. " Yes. . . ."

And she relapsed into the wealth of memories of . . . . what ? Once before, in this way, she had walked along these same paths, past these jasmine vines, so long, so long ago ; had walked with him, with him. . . . Why ? Was the past repeating itself after centuries. . . . ?

"It is three weeks since you came to see me," she said, simply, recovering herself.

"Forgive me," he replied.

"What was the reason?"

He hesitated, seeking an excuse.

"I don't know," he answered, softly. "You forgive me, do you not? One day it was this, another day that. And then .... I don't know. Many reasons together. It is not good that I should see you often. Not good for you, nor for me."

"Let us begin with the second. Why is it not good for you?"

"No, let us begin with the first: with what concerns you. People...."

"People?"

"People are talking about us. I am looked upon as an irretrievable rake. I will not have your name linked profanely with mine."

" And is it ? "

" Yes. . . ."

She smiled.

" I do not mind."

" But you must mind; if not for your own
sake. . . ."

He stopped. She knew he was thinking of
her boys; she shrugged her shoulders.

" And now, why is it not good for you ? "

" One should not be happy too often."

" What a sophism !   Why not ? "

" I do not know; but I feel I am right.   It
spoils one; it blunts the appetite."

" Are you happy here, then ? "

He smiled, and nodded yes.

They were silent a long time.   They were
sitting at the end of the garden, upon a seat that
stood in a semi-circle of rhododendrons in flower;
the great blossoms of purple satin shut them in

with a high wall of closely clustered bouquets, rising from the paths and overtopping their heads; clambering roses flung their incense before them. They sat still, happy together, happy in the sympathy of their atmospheres mingling together; yet in their happiness there was the invincible melancholy which is an integral part of all life, even in happiness.

"I do not know how I am to tell you," he resumed; "but suppose I were to see you every day, every moment that I thought of you. . . . That would not do. For then I should become so refined, so subtle, that from pure happiness I should not be able to live; my other being would receive nothing, and suffer hunger like a beast. I am bad, I am egotistical to be able to speak like this, but I must tell you the truth, that you may not think too well of me. So I only seek your society as something beautiful

above all things, with which I indulge myself
only on rare occasions."

She was silent.

"Sometimes . . . . sometimes, too, I think that
in doing this I am not doing right so far as you
are concerned; that in some way or other I
offend or hurt you. Then I sit thinking about
it, until I feel sure it would be best to take leave
of you for ever."

She was silent still; motionless she sat, with
her hands listlessly in her lap, her head slightly
bowed, a smile about her mouth.

"Speak to me. . . ." he begged.

"You do not offend me, nor hurt me," she
said. "Come to me whenever you feel the need.
Do always as you think best, and I shall think
that best too; you must not doubt that."

"I should so much like to know in what way
you like me?"

"In what way? Surely, as a madonna a sinner who repents and gives her his soul," she said, archly. "Am I not a madonna?"

"Are you content to be so?"

"Can you be so ignorant about women not to know how in each one of us there is a longing to solace and relieve, to play, in fact, at being a madonna?"

"Do not speak so," he said, with pain in his voice.

"I am speaking seriously. . . ."

He looked at her; a doubt rose within him, but she smiled to him; a calm glory was about her; she sat amidst the bouquets of the rhododendrons as in the blossom-bosom of one great mystic flower. The wound of his doubt was soothed with balsam. He gave himself up wholly to his happiness; an atmosphere wafted about them of the sweet calm of life, an atmosphere

in which life becomes dispassionate and restful
and smiling, like the air which is rare about the
gods. It began to grow dark; a violet gloom
fell from the sky like crape falling upon crape;
quietly the stars lighted out. The shadows in
the garden, between the shrubs among which
they sat, flowed into one another; the piano in
the adjacent villa had stopped. And Happiness
drew a veil between his soul and the outside
world: the garden with its design of plots and
paths; the villa with curtains at its windows, and
its iron gate; the road behind, with the rattle
of carriages and trams. All this withdrew itself
far back; all ordinary life retreated far from him;
vanishing behind the veil, it died away. It was
no dream nor conceit: reality to him was the
Happiness that had come while the world died
away; the Happiness that was rare, invisible,
intangible, coming from the Love which alone

is sympathy, calm and without passion, the Love which exists purely of itself, without further thought either of taking anything, or even of giving anything, the love of the gods, that is the soul of Love itself. High he felt himself: the like of the illusion he had of her, which she wished to maintain for his sake, of which he was now absolutely certain, doubting nothing. For he could not understand that what had given him happiness—his illusion—so perfect, so crystalline, could cause her any grief; he could not at this moment penetrate without sin into the truth of the law which insists on equilibrium, which takes away from one what it offers another, which gives Happiness and Grief together; he could not understand that if Happiness was with him, with her there was anguish, anguish that she must make a pretence and deceive him for his own sake : anguish that she wanted above all

what was earthly, that she craved for what was
earthly, panted for earthly pleasures. . . . ! Still
less could he know that, through all this, there
was voluptuousness in her anguish : that to suffer
through him, to suffer for him, made of her
anguish all voluptuousness.

II.

It was dark and late, and still they sat
there.

" Shall we go for a walk ? " she asked.

He hesitated, but she asked anew, " Why not,
if you care to ? "

And he could no longer refuse.

They rose up, and went along by the back of
the house ; Cecile said to the maid, whom she
saw sitting sewing by the kitchen door :

" Greta, fetch me my small black hat, my
black lace shawl, and a pair of gloves."

The servant rose and went into the house.

Cecile noticed how a little shyness marked itself more strongly in Quaerts' hesitation now that they were waiting between the flower beds. She smiled, plucked a rose, and placed it in her waistband.

"Have the boys gone to bed?" he asked.

"Yes," she replied, still smiling, "long ago."

The servant returned; Cecile put on the small black hat and the lace about her neck; she refused the gloves Greta offered her.

"No, not these; get me a pair of grey ones. . . ."

The servant went into the house again, and as Cecile looked at Quaerts her gaiety increased; she gave a little laugh.

"What is the matter?" she asked, mischievously, knowing perfectly what it was.

"Nothing, nothing!" he said, vaguely, and waited patiently until Greta returned.

Then they went through the garden gate into the woods. They walked slowly, without speaking; Cecile played with her long gloves, not putting them on.

" Really. . . . " he began, hesitating.

" Come, what is it ? "

" You know; I told you the other day; it is not right. . . . "

" What ? "

" What we are doing now. You risk too much."

" Too much, with you ? "

" If any one were to see us. . . . "

" And what then ? "

He shook his head.

" You are wilful; you know very well."

She clinched her eyes; her mouth grew serious; she pretended to be a little angry.

" Listen, you must not be anxious if I am not.

I am doing no harm. Our walks are not secret; Greta at least knows about them. And, besides, I am free to do as I please."

"It is my fault; the first time we went for a walk in the evening it was at my request. . . ."

"Then do penance and be good; come now, without scruple, at *my* request. . . . " she said, with mock emphasis.

He yielded, too happy to wish to make any sacrifice to a convention which at that moment did not exist.

They walked silently. Cecile's sensations came to her always in shocks of surprise. So it had been when Jules had grown suddenly angry with her; so also, midway on the stair, after that conversation at dinner of circles of sympathy. And now, precisely in the same way, with the shock of sudden revelation, came this new sensation—that after all she did not suffer so seriously

as she had at first thought; that her agony,
being voluptuousness, could not be a martyrdom;
that she was happy, that Happiness had come
about her in the fine air of his atmosphere, because they were together, together. . . . Oh, why
wish for anything more, above all for things less
pure? Did he not love her, and was not his love
already a fact, and was it not on a sufficiently
low plane now that it was an absolute fact?
Did he not love her with a tenderness which
feared for anything which might trouble her in
the world, through her ignoring it and wandering
with him alone in the dark? Did he not love
her with tenderness, but also with the lustre of
the divinity of his soul, calling her madonna, by
this title making her—unconsciously, perhaps, in
his simplicity—the equal of all that was divine
in him? Did he not love her, did he not?
Why did she want more? No, no, she wanted

nothing more; she was happy, she shared Happiness with him; he gave it her just as she gave
it him; it was a sphere that progressed with
them, as they walked together, seeking their
way along the darkling paths of the woods, she
leaning on his arm, he leading her, for she could
see nothing in the dark; which yet was not dark,
but pure light of their Happiness. And so it
was as if it was not evening, but day, noon;
noon in the night, hour of bright light in the
dusk!

III.

And the darkness was light; the night dawned
into Light which beamed on every side. Calmly
it beamed, the Light, like one solitary sunstar,
beaming with the soft lustre of purity, bright in
a heaven of still, white, silver air; a heaven where
they walked along milky ways of light and music;
it beamed and sounded beneath their feet; it

13

welled in seas of ether high above their heads, and beamed and sounded there, high and clear. And they were alone in their heaven, in their infinite heaven, which was all space, endless beneath them and above and around them, endless spaces of light and music, of light that was music. Their heaven measured itself on every side with blessed perspectives of white radiance, fading away in lustre and swooning landscape; oases of flowers and plants by watersides of light, still and clear and hush with peace. For its peace was the ether in which all desire is dissolved and becomes of crystal, and their life in it was the limpid existence in unruffled peace; they walked on, in heavenly sympathy of fellowship, close together, hemmed in one narrow circle, one circle of radiance which embraced them. Barely was there a recollection in them of the world which had died out in the glitter of

their heaven ; there was nothing in them but the
ecstasy of their love, which had become their soul,
as if they no longer had any soul, were only love;
and when they looked about them and upon the
Light, they saw that their heaven, in which their
Happiness was the Light, was nothing but their
love ; and that the landscapes—the flowers and
plants by watersides of light—were nothing but
their love, and that the endless space, the eterni-
ties of lustre and music, measuring themselves
out on every hand, beneath them and above and
· around them, were nothing but their love, which
had grown into heaven and happiness.

And now they came into the very midst, to the
very sun-centre, the very goal which Cecile had
once foreseen, concealed in the distance, in the
outbeaming of innate divinity. Up to the
very goal they stepped, and all around it shot
its endless rays into space unspanned, as if

their Love were becoming the centre of the universe. . . .

IV.

They sat on a bench, in the dark, not knowing that it was dark, for their eyes were full of the Light. They sat against one another, silently at first, till, remembering that he had a voice and could still speak words, he said :

" I have never lived through such a moment as this. I forget where we are, and who we are, and that we are human. We have been so, have we not; I remember that we were so ? "

" Yes, but now we are no longer," she said, smiling ; and her eyes, grown big, looked into the darkness that was Light.

" Once we were human, suffering and desiring, in a world where certainly much was beautiful, but much also was ugly."

" Why speak of that now ? " she asked, and

her voice sounded to herself as coming from very far and low beneath her.

" I remembered it. . . ."

" I wish to forget it."

" Then I will also. But I may thank you in human speech that you have lifted me above humanity ? "

" Have I done so ? "

" Yes ; may I thank you for that . . . . on my knees ? "

He knelt down and reverently took her hands. He could just distinguish the silhouette of her figure, still, seated motionless upon the bench ; above them was a pearl-grey twilight of stars, between the black boughs. She felt her hands in his, and his mouth, a kiss, upon her hand. Gently she released herself; and then, with a great soul of modesty, full of desireless happiness, she very gently bent her arms about his neck, took his head against her, and kissed his forehead.

" And I, I thank you too!" she whispered, rapturously.

He was still, and she held him fast in her embrace.

" I thank you," she said, " that you have taught me this and how to be happy as we are, and not otherwise. You see, when I still lived, and was human, a woman, I thought I had already lived before I met you, for I had had a husband, and children of whom I was very fond. But from you I first learnt to live, to live without egoism and without desire; I learnt that from you this evening or .... this day, which is it? You have given me life, and happiness, and everything. And I thank you, I thank you! You see, you are so great and so strong and so clear, and you have borne me towards your own

Happiness, which should also be mine, but it was so far above me that without you I should never have attained it! For there was a barrier for me which did not exist for you. You see, when I was still human,"—and she laughed, clasping him more tightly—" I had a sister, and she too felt there was a barrier between her happiness and herself; and she felt she could not surmount this barrier, and was so unhappy because of it that she feared lest she should go mad. But I, I do not know: I dreamed, I thought, I hoped, I waited, oh! I waited, and then you came, and you made me understand at once that you could be no man, no husband for me, but that you could be more for me: my angel, O my deliverer, who should take me in his arms and bear me up over the barrier into his own heaven, where he himself was master, and make me his queen. Oh, I thank you, I thank you! I do not know how to thank you; I can only say that I love you, that I adore you, that I lay myself at your feet. Remain so, and let me adore you, while you kneel where you are. I may adore you, may I not, while you yourself kneel? You see I too must confess, as you used to do," she continued, for now she could not but confess. "I have not always been straightforward with you; I have sometimes pretended to be the madonna, knowing all the time I was but an ordinary woman, a woman who frankly loved you. But I deceived you for your own happiness, did I not? You wished me so, you were happy when I was so and not otherwise. And now, now too you must forgive me, because now I need no longer pretend, because that is past and gone away, because I myself have died away from myself, because now I am no longer a woman, no longer human for myself, but only what you wish me to be: a madonna and your creature, an atom of your own essence and divinity. Do you then forgive me the past ? .... May I thank you for my happiness, for my heaven, my light, O my master, for my joy, my great, my immeasurably great joy ? "

He rose and sat beside her, taking her gently in his arms.

"Are you happy ? " he asked.

"Yes," she said, laying her head on his shoulder in a giddiness of light. "And you ? "

"Yes," he answered, and he asked again : "And do you desire .... nothing more ? "

"Nothing ! " she stammered. " I want nothing but this, nothing but what is mine, oh, nothing, nothing more ! "

"Swear it to me then .... by something sacred ! "

" I swear it to you . . . . by yourself ! "

He pressed her head to his shoulder again.
He smiled, and she did not see that there was
melancholy in his laugh, for she was blind with
light.

V.

They were long silent, sitting there. She
knew she had said many things, she no longer
knew what. About her she saw that it was
dark, with only that pearl-grey twilight of stars
above their heads, between the black boughs.
She felt that she lay with her head on his
shoulder; she heard his breath. A sort of chill
ran down her shoulders, notwithstanding the
warmth of his embrace; she drew the lace closer
about her throat, and felt that the bench on
which they sat was moist with dew.

" I thank you, I love you so, you make me so
happy," she repeated.

He was silent; he pressed her to him very gently, with simple tenderness. Her last words still sounded in her ears after she had spoken them. Then she was bound to acknowledge to herself that they had not been spontaneous, like all that she had told him before, as he lay kneeling before her with his head at her breast. She had spoken them to break the silence: formerly that silence had never troubled her, why should it now?

"Come!" he said gently, and even yet she did not hear the melancholy in his voice, in this single word.

They rose, and walked on. It came to him that it was late, that they must return by the same path; beyond that his thought was sad with things he could not have uttered; a poor twilight had come about him after the blinding Light of their heaven of just before. He had to be cautious: it was very dark, and he could barely see the path, hesitating, very pale at their feet; they brushed the trunks of the trees as they passed.

" I can see nothing," said Cecile, laughing. " Can you see the way ? "

" Rely upon me; I can see quite well in the dark," he replied. " I am lynx-eyed. . . ."

Step by step they went on, and she felt a sweet joy in being guided by him; she clasped his arm more closely, saying laughingly that she was afraid, and that she would be terrified if he were suddenly to leave hold of her.

" And supposing I were suddenly to run away and leave you alone ? " said Quaerts.

She laughed; she besought him not to do so. Then she was silent, angry with herself for laughing; a weight of melancholy bore her down because of her jesting and laughter. She felt as if she were unworthy of that to which, in radiant light, she had just been received.

And in him, too, there was melancholy : the melancholy that he had to lead her through the darkness, by invisible paths, by rows of invisible tree-trunks which might graze and wound her ; that he had to lead her through a dark wood, through a black sea, through an ink-dark sphere, returning from a heaven where all had been light and all happiness, without melancholy, or any darkness.

And so they were silent in their melancholy until they reached the high road, the old Scheveningen Road.

They approached the villa. A tram went by ; two or three people passed on foot ; it was a fine evening. He brought her back and waited until the door opened to his ring. The door remained unopened ; meantime he pressed her hand tightly, and involuntarily he hurt her a little. Greta had no doubt fallen asleep.

" Ring again, would you ? "

He rang again, louder ; after a moment the door opened. She gave him her hand a second time, with a smile.

"Good-night, mevrouw," he said, taking her fingers respectfully, and raising his hat.

Now, now she could hear the sound of his voice, the note in it of melancholy. . . .

CHAPTER V.

I.

She knew, the next day, when she sat alone in reflection, that the sphere of happiness, the highest and brightest, may not be trod; that it may only beam upon us as a sun, and that we may not enter into it, into the holy sun-centre. They had done that. . . .

Listless she sat, her children by her side, Christie looking pale and languid. Yes, she spoiled them, but how could she change herself?

Weeks passed, and Cecile heard nothing from Quaerts. It was always so: after he had been with her, weeks would drag by without her ever seeing him. He was much too happy with her, it was too much for him. He looked upon her society as a rare pleasure to be very jealously indulged in. And she, she loved him simply, with the devoutest essence of her soul, loved him frankly, as a woman loves a man. . . . She always wanted him, every day, every hour, at every pulse of her life.

Then she met him by chance at Scheveningen, one evening when she went down there with Amélie and Suzette. Then once again at a reception at Mrs. Hoze's. He seemed shy with her, and a certain pride in her forbade her asking him to call. Yes, some change had come over what had been woven between them. But she suffered sorely, because of that foolish pride, because she had not humbly begged him to come to her. But was he not her idol? What he did was good.

So she did not see him for weeks, weeks.

Life went on; each day she had her little occupations, in her household, with her children; Mrs. Hoze reproached her for her sequestration from society, and she began to think more about her friends, to please Mrs. Hoze, who had asked this. There were vistas in her memory; in those vistas she saw the dinner-party, their conversations and walks, all their love, all his aspiration to her he called madonna; their last evening of light and ecstasy. Then she smiled, and the smile itself beamed over her anguish; her anguish that she no longer saw him, that she felt proud and had bitterness within her. Yet all things must be well, as he wished them.

Oh, the evenings, the summer evenings, cooling after the warm days, the evenings when she sat alone, peering out from her room, where the onyx lamp burnt with a half flame,

peering out of the open windows at the trams
which, tinkling their bells, came and went to
Scheveningen, full, full of people. Waiting, the
endless long waiting, evening after evening in
solitude, after the children had gone to bed.
Waiting, when she simply sat still, staring
fixedly before her, looking at the trams, the
tedious, everlasting trams. Where was her
former evenness of dreaming happiness ? And
where, where was her supreme happiness ? Where
was her struggle within herself between what
she was and what he thought she was ? This
struggle no longer existed; this had been
overcome ; she no longer felt the force of
passion ; she only longed for him as he had
always come, as he now no longer came. Why
did he not come ? Happiness palled, people
spoke about them. . . . It was not right that
they should see much of one another—he

had said so the evening before that highest happiness—not good for him and not good for her.

So she sat and thought, and great quiet tears fell from her eyes, for she knew that although he remained away partly on his own account, it was above all on hers that he did not come to her. What had she not said to him that evening on the bench in the woods, when her arms were about his neck? Oh! she should have been silent, she knew that now. She should not have uttered her rapture, but have enjoyed it secretly within herself; she should have let him utter himself; she herself should have remained his madonna. But she had been too full, too happy, and in that overbrimming of happiness she had been unable to be other than true and clear as a bright mirror. He had glanced into her and comprehended her entirely: she knew that, she was certain of that.

He knew now in what manner she loved him; she herself had revealed it to him. But, at the same time, she had made known to him all that was past, that now she was what he wished her to be. And this had been true at that moment, clear at that moment, and true. . . . But now? Does ecstasy endure only for one moment then, and did he know it? Did he know that her soul's flight had reached its limit, and must now descend again to a commoner sphere? Did he know that she loved him again now, quite ordinarily, with all her being, wholly and entirely, no longer as widely as the heavens, only as widely as her arms could stretch out and embrace? And could he not return her this love, so petty, and was that why he did not come to her?

II.

Then she received his letter :

" Forgive me that I put off from day to day coming to see you ; forgive me that even to-day I cannot decide to do so, and that I write to you instead. Forgive me if I even venture to ask you whether it may not be necessary that we see each other no more. If I hurt you and offend you, if I—God spare me —cause you to suffer, forgive me, forgive me. Perhaps I procrastinated a little from indecision, but much more because I thought I had no other choice.

" There has been between our two lives, between our two souls, a rare moment of happiness which was a special blessedness, a special grace. Do you not think so too? Oh, if only I had words to tell you how thankful I am in my innermost soul for that happiness. If later I ever look back upon my life, I shall always continue to see that happiness gleaming in between the ugliness and the blackness—a star of light. We received it as such—a gift of light. And I venture to ask you if that gift is not a thing to be kept sacred?

"Shall we be able to do so if I continue to see you? You, yes, I have no doubt of you; you will be strong to keep it sacred, our blessed happiness, especially as you have already done battle, as you confided to me, that holy evening. But I, shall I too be able to be strong, especially now that I know that you have gone through the struggle? I doubt myself, I doubt my own force; I am afraid of myself. There is cruelty in me, the love of destruction, something of the savage. As a boy I took pleasure in destroying beautiful things, in breaking and soiling them. The other day Jules brought me some roses to my room; in the evening, as I sat alone, thinking upon you and upon our happiness—yes, at that very moment—my fingers began to fumble with a rose whose petals were loose, and when I saw that one rose dispetaled there came a rage within me to tear and destroy them all, and I rumpled every one of them. I only give you small instances, I do not wish to give a larger instance, from vanity, lest you should know how bad I am. I am afraid of myself. If I saw you again, and again, and again, what should I begin to feel and think and wish, unconsciously? Which would be the stronger within me, my soul or the beast that is in me? Forgive me that I lay bare my dread before you, and do not despise me for it. Up to the present I have *not* done battle in the blessed world of our happiness. I saw you, I saw you often before I knew you; I imagined you as you were; I was allowed to speak to you; it was given me to love you with

my soul alone : I beseech you let it remain so.
Let me continue to guard my happiness like this,
to keep it sacred, a thousand times sacred. I
think it worth while to have lived now that I
have known that : happiness, the highest. I am
afraid of the battle which would probably come
and pollute that sacred thing.

"Will you believe me when I swear to you
that I have reflected deeply on all this? Will
you believe me when I swear to you that I suffer
at the thought of never being permitted to see
you again ? Above all, will you forgive me when
I swear to you that I am acting in this way
because I think I am doing right? Oh! I am
thankful to you, and I love you as a soul of light
alone, only light !

"Perhaps I do wrong to send you this letter.
I do not know. Perhaps I will presently destroy
what I have written. . . ."

Yet he had sent the letter.

There was bitterness within her. She had done battle once, had conquered herself, and in a sacred moment had confessed both battle and conquest; she knew that fate had compelled her to do so; she now knew that through this confession she would lose him. For a short moment, a single evening perhaps, she had been worthy of her god, and his equal. Now she was so no longer; for that reason too she felt bitter; and bitterest of all because the thought dared to rise within her:

"A god! Is he a god? Is a god afraid of battle?"

Then her threefold bitterness changed to despair, black despair, a night which her eyes sought to penetrate in order to see where they saw nothing, nothing, and she moaned low, and wrung her hands, sunk into a heap before the

window, and peering at the trams which, with
the tinkling of their bells, ran pitilessly to and
fro.

III.

She shut herself up; she saw little of her
children; she told her friends that she was ill.
She was at home to no visitors. She guessed
intuitively that in their respective circles people
spoke of Quaerts and herself. Life hung dull
about her, a closely woven web of tiresome
meshes, and she remained motionless in her
corner, to avoid entangling herself in those
meshes. Once Jules forced his way to her; he
went up to her in spite of Greta's protests; he
sought her in the little boudoir, and, not finding
her, went resolutely to her bedroom. He knocked
without receiving any reply, but entered nevertheless. The room was half in darkness, for she
kept the blinds lowered; in the shadow of the

canopy which rose above the bedstead, with its hangings of old-blue brocade, Cecile lay sleeping. Her dressing-gown was open over her breast, the train fell from the bed and lay creased over the carpet; her hair trailed over the pillows; one of her hands clutched nervously at the tulle bed-curtain.

"Auntie!" cried Jules. "Auntie!"

He shook her by the arm, and she waked heavily, with heavy, blue-encircled eyes. She did not recognise him at first, and thought that he was little Dolf.

"It is I, auntie; Jules. . . ."

She recognised him, asked him how he came there, what was the matter, whether he did not know that she was ill?

"I knew, but I wanted to speak to you. I came to speak to you about . . . . him. . . ."

"Him?"

" About Taco.   He asked me to tell you.   He
could not write to you, he said.   He is going on
a long journey with his friend from Brussels; he
will be away a long time, and he would like . . . .
he would like to take leave of you."

" To take leave ? "

" Yes, and he told me to ask you whether he
might see you once more ? "

She had half risen up, and looked at Jules
stupidly.   In an instant the memory ran through
her brain of a long look which Jules directed on
her so strangely when she saw Quaerts for the
first time and spoke to him coolly and distantly :
' Have you many relations in the Hague ?   You
have no occupation I believe? Sport? Oh!' . . . .
The memory of Jules playing on the piano, of
Rubinstein's Romance in Es, of the ecstasy of his
fantasia : the glittering rainbows and the souls
turning to angels.

" To take leave ? " she repeated.

Jules nodded. " Yes, auntie, he is going away for a long, long time."

He could have shed tears himself, and there were tears in his voice, but he would not, and his eyes were moist.

" He told me to ask you," he repeated with difficulty.

" Whether he can come and take leave ? "

" Yes, auntie."

She made no reply, but lay staring before her. An emptiness began to measure itself out before her, in endless perspective, a silhouette of their evening of rapture, but no light beamed out of the shadow.

" Emptiness. . . ." she muttered through closed lips.

" What, auntie ? "

She would have liked to ask Jules whether he

was still, as formerly, afraid of the emptiness within himself; but a gentleness of pity, a soft feeling, a sweetening of the bitterness which so filled her being, stayed her.

"To take leave?" she repeated, with a smile of melancholy, and the big tears fell heavily, drop by drop, upon her fingers wrung together.

" Yes, auntie. . . ."

He could no longer restrain himself: a single sob convulsed his throat, but he gave a cough to conceal it. Cecile threw her arm round his neck.

" You are very fond of .... Taco, are you not?" she asked; and it struck her that this was the first time she had pronounced the name, for she had never called Quaerts by it : she had never called him by any name.

He did not answer at first, but nestled in her arm, in her embrace, and began to cry.

"Yes; I cannot tell you how much," he said.

"I know," she said, and she thought of the rainbows and the angels; he had played as out of her own soul.

"May he come?" asked Jules, faithfully thoughtful of his instructions.

"Yes."

"He asks whether he may come this evening?"

"Very well."

"Auntie, he is going away, because .... because. . . ."

"Because what, Jules?"

"Because of you; because you do not like him, and will not marry him. Mamma says so. . . ."

She made no reply; she lay sobbing, her head on Jules' head.

"Is it true, auntie? No, it is not true, is it . . . . ?"

" No."

" Why, then ? "

She raised herself suddenly, conquering herself, and looked at him fixedly.

" He is going away because he must, Jules. I cannot tell you why. But what he does is right. All that he does is right."

The boy looked at her, motionless, with large wet eyes, full of astonishment.

" Is right ? " he repeated.

" Yes. He is better than any of us. If you continue to love him, Jules, it will bring you happiness, even if . . . . if you never see him again."

" Do you think so ? " he asked. " Does he bring happiness ? Even in that case. . . . "

" Even in that case. . . . "

She listened to her words as she spoke them : it was to her as if another was speaking ; another who consoled not only Jules but herself as well, and who would perhaps give her strength to take leave from Taco as would be seemly— without despair.

IV.

"So you are going a long journey?" she asked.

He sat facing her, motionless, with anguish on his face. Outwardly she was very calm, only there was melancholy in her look and in her voice. In her white dress, with the girdle falling before her feet, she lay back among the three cushions of the rose-moiré *chaise-longue*; the points of her little slippers were lost in the sheepskin rug. On the little table before her lay a great bouquet of loose roses, pink, white, and yellow, bound together with a broad riband. He had brought them for her,

15

and she had not yet placed them. There was great calm about her ; the " exquisite" atmosphere of the boudoir seemed unchanged.

"Tell me, do I not grieve you sorely ? " he asked, with the anguish in his eyes, the eyes she now knew so well.

She smiled.

" No. . . ." she said. " I will be honest with you. I have suffered, but I suffer no longer. I have battled with myself for the second time, and I have conquered myself. Will you believe me ? "

" If you knew the remorse that I feel. . . ."

She rose and went to him.

" Why ? " she asked in a clear voice. " Because you comprehended me, and gave me happiness ? "

" Did I do so ? "

" Have you forgotten, then ? "

" No, but I thought. . . ."

" What ? "

" I do not know ; thought that you would—
would suffer so, I . . . . I cursed myself. . . .! "

She shook her head gently, with smiling
disapproval.

" For shame ! " she said. " Do not blas-
pheme. . . ."

" Can you forgive me ? "

" I have nothing to forgive. Listen to me.
Swear to me that you believe me, that you
believe that you have given me happiness and
that I am not suffering."

" I . . . . I swear."

" I trust you do not swear this merely to
comply with my wish."

" You have been the highest in my life,"
he said, gently.

A rapture shot through her soul.

" Tell me only. . . ." she began.

" What ? "

" Tell me if you believe that I, I, *I* . . . . shall always remain the highest in your life."

She stood before him, tall, in her clinging white. She seemed to shed radiance; never yet had he seen her so beautiful.

" I am certain of that," he said. " Certain, oh! certain. . . . My God! how can I convey the certainty of it to you ? "

" But I believe you, I believe you," she exclaimed.

She laughed a laugh of rapture. In her soul a sun seemed to be shooting out rays on every side. She placed her arm tenderly about his neck and kissed his forehead, a caress of chastity.

For one moment he seemed to forget everything. He too rose, took her in his arms, almost savagely, and clasped her suddenly to him, as if he were about to crush her against his breast. She just caught sight of his sad eyes, and then nothing more, blinded by the kisses of his mouth, which rained upon her whole face in sparks of fire. With the sun-rapture of her soul was mingled a bliss of earth, a yielding to the violence of his embrace. She released herself, put him away, and said :

" And now . . . . go."

It stunned him ; he understood that to be final.

" Yes, yes, I am going," he said. " I may write to you, may I not ? "

She nodded yes, with her smile.

" Write to me, I will write to you too," she said. " Let me always hear from you. . . ."

" Then these are not to be the last words between us ? This . . . . this . . . . is not the end ? "

"No. . . ."

"Thank you. Good-bye, mevrouw, good-bye
. . . . Cecile. Ah! if you knew what this
moment costs me!"

"It must be. It cannot be otherwise. Go,
go. You must go. Do go. . . ."

She gave her hand again, for the last time.
A moment later he was gone.

She looked strangely about her, with be-
wildered eyes, with hands locked together.
"Go, go. . . ." she repeated, like one raving.
Then she noticed the roses. With a light
scream she sank down before the little table and
buried her face in his gift, until the thorns
wounded her face. The pain—two drops of blood
which fell from her forehead—brought her back
to her senses. Standing before the little Venetian mirror hanging over her writing-table, she

wiped away the red spots with her handkerchief.

" Happiness ! " she stammered to herself. " His happiness! The highest in his life! So he knew happiness, though short it was. But now .... now he suffers, now he will suffer again as before. The remembrance of happiness cannot do everything. Ah! if it could only do that, then everything would be well, everything .... I wish for nothing more, I have had my life, my own life, my own happiness ; I have now my children; I belong to them now. To him I was not permitted to be anything more. . . ."

She turned away from the mirror and sat down on the settee, as if tired with a great space traversed ; and she closed her eyes, as if stunned with too great a light. She folded her hands together like one in prayer ; her face beamed in its fatigue from smile to smile.

" Happiness ! " she repeated, falteringly. "The highest in his life! O my God, happiness! I thank Thee, O God, I thank Thee. . . ."

THE END.